FINDING PAIGE

RENEE SCARROTT

Sky Ranch
PUBLISHING

Library of Congress Control Number 2023917126

ISBN: 979-8-9891132-1-7 (pbk.)
ISBN: 979-8-9891132-3-1 (e-book)

Printed in the United States of America

JR Sky Ranch Publishing
South Dakota

Cover design by
Vivien Reis

For all the dreamers who believe the world is full of magical things. It is the bridge that takes us from the visible to the invisible, as only when we experience the magic do we experience the extraordinary.

FINDING PAIGE

1

I awoke disoriented and paused to untangle my thoughts.
Was I dreaming? I felt anxious, and the day hadn't even begun yet. Mornings like this weren't unusual for me around this time of year. Maybe I was just sleep-deprived knowing the events that had taken place leading up to this day . . . I could see her face so clearly! It was as if she were still there with me, trying to tell me something, as though she was crying out that she was right in front of me! I wanted to tell her I had searched for so long but couldn't find her. I didn't want to wake up, feeling as if I did, I wouldn't find out what had happened to her. As hard as I tried to find out in my dreams, I always woke before she could tell me.

I closed my eyes, trying to make sense of it all, the thoughts swirling around in my head, wishing I could sink back into the warmth of my covers. Without looking at the calendar, I already knew what day it was. It was Friday, August 10. It was a day that marked the beginning of a tragedy surrounded by a mystery that had followed me for much of my life. On this day twenty-two years ago, my best friend Paige disappeared and was never heard from again. Not a day had gone by that I hadn't thought of her. Paige and I were inseparable and met when we were eight years old.

At the time, my father accepted a promotion as the new head coach of Bayfield, Florida's Sycamore Cove varsity football team. It meant moving away from our life in Gainesville, Georgia, which was all I had ever known. We were a family, just my father and me. My mother had passed away two years prior from a rare form of lung cancer. That year leading up to my mother's death had been traumatic, and being so young, I don't remember much of her suffering, which in many ways was a blessing in disguise.

My sorrow was cloaked in the vague smog of early half-remembered maternal warmth, lacking any cruelty of the realities of her condition. I wished so badly that I could see her just one more time. I recall calling for her to tuck me in as I eagerly waited for her to read me one of my favorite princess stories for bedtime. She always ended the story with a gentle kiss on my forehead and whispered, "Goodnight, my angel. Sweet dreams. Mama loves you." The words were so clear in my head, but her face was a blur. Remembering my mother was a mixture of nostalgia and sorrow that I tried to avoid but never could. My heart still longed for her.

The years had taken an indescribable toll on my father, Simon. The happy-go-lucky, stalwart man I had always known as my father had been replaced with a man who was always anxious, worried, and solemn. He never talked about my mother or her passing, which I guess was his way of coping with the overwhelming grief of losing someone he loved. At the time, I believed he must have wanted to move on, which is why he accepted the offer in Bayfield, as difficult as the decision must have been. Looking back, I believe he wanted to make a fresh start for us both, but I admit it made me resentful. Bayfield was only five hours away from Gainesville, but it seemed like it was on the other side of the world.

"You'll love the new school, Olivia, and I'm sure you'll make new friends there." He waited for my response, catching my gaze with a valiant smile of bravery. Even then, I knew that the smile was just there for me and was a gesture to put me at ease. It was hard to counter or fight back at anything my father said, as I could still feel the overwhelming pain he was bearing from losing my mother, Camila. If he could be brave, then I wanted to be brave, too, but I couldn't look directly into his eyes. My gaze fell on my pretty pink nails. Oh, how they glistened in the soft glow of the lamplight. I knew he would look through my brave facade and see the fear that continued running rampant within me. "Just be brave," I thought as I fought back tears.

"I know, Daddy."

I didn't want to live in a new house or go to a new school, but despite my feelings or reservations, moving day soon came, and we quickly settled into our new home. I remember that first day following the move like it was yesterday. The following morning, I decided to explore the neighborhood on foot as my father worked on organizing the stacks of storage boxes. I felt like I needed to look around to prove the reality of my new surroundings to myself. Dad had looked at me with a smile. "Be back in half an hour, Olivia, and don't wander too far." Despite the smile, there was no mirth or warmth in his voice, and I knew he must have been dealing with the emotions of the move in his own way.

"I won't, Daddy. I promise."

The rays of sunlight washed over me as I set out to explore my new surroundings. My long brown hair continued to whip about my face as I skipped clumsily down the street. I suddenly came across a posted sign just a few houses down that offered a narrow walking trail leading to a public park. This was the first thing I remember being truly happy about in my new home. Gainesville hadn't had something like this, at least not where I had lived. I decided to explore the path, thinking it would be much faster than taking the main road, and excited to see where it would lead.

I continued to glance at my watch as I followed the path, checking the time, trying to pay attention to the time limit my dad had given me. When I looked up, I gasped, as the most majestic lake I had ever seen was surrounded by a raft of white-crested ducks that called the tranquil waters their home. I was immediately drawn to its divine grandeur and envisioned the bright blue water enveloping me, feeling at peace, if only for the moment the daydream lasted. I wanted to stay there, basking in its bliss. A sense of dreamy calmness washed over me as I felt myself almost floating on the trail back home.

Just as I arrived and started helping my father organize the kitchen, I thought I heard a faint tapping sound; it was quick and rhythmic. The sound grew louder as I followed it to the front door. I opened it, only to see a young girl standing there, a smile on her face. "Hi, I'm Paige Phillips, and I live next door. I saw you moving in and wanted to meet you. What's your name?"

I don't know how long I stood there, mesmerized by her presence. She had an angelic face, with thick dark eyelashes and rosy cheeks. She nervously twirled her long golden hair as her sparkling pink nail polish flashed through her silky strands. Her piercing blue eyes were enchanting. One could get lost in them and be forever changed. Perhaps it's the goggles of nostalgia, but I distinctly remember our first meeting as a dreamlike, idyllic event.

I heard myself say, "Hi, I'm Olivia Monroe." That was the day that forever changed my life. Paige almost immediately became my best friend. We were utterly inseparable. By a stroke of luck, we were even in the same third-grade class together. Our teacher, Mrs. Myers, constantly had to reprimand us for making funny faces and giggling during class time. Looking back, I'm not sure why we weren't separated in the classroom, but I'm glad we weren't. Every day after school, we would take the bus home and rush over to each other's houses. Most of the time, I would find myself at her house since she had all the pretty things any girl could ever ask for.

Paige always got what she wanted, although I never thought anything of it then since she always shared everything with me. If we were home on the weekends, I would almost always hear her calling my name from her bedroom window. "Livvy, can you come over and play dress-up?" She was always excited to show me the latest princess dress and glitter makeup her mother had bought her.

Knowing I had lost my mother, she was sometimes hesitant about wearing her newest dresses in front of me, always telling me to try them on first. Sometimes, her mother, Betty, would buy identical dresses for us. I felt a great sense of family and kinship around Paige. She was like a sister to me. When I was expected home, I would walk in the door with the prettiest pink nails, the reddest rouge on my cheeks, and usually lipstick to match.

My father would shake his head and chuckle. I know that deep down he loved Paige like a daughter and was happy I had someone my age around whom I felt so connected to. I think seeing me so happy gave him some of his life back. He was still like a different man, but at least there was some of that warmth that I remembered. He would sometimes take us to get ice cream cones at the local drugstore, and he always let us get two scoops. It was like hitting the jackpot for two eight-year-olds. Two scoops of rocky road with your best friend; life doesn't get much better at that age. Paige's sweet smile was always contagious. She affected everyone she was around. People would always smile back at her warmly, as though she were their daughter or close friend. She just had an infectious type of spirit. It could be felt by simply being in her presence, just like I had experienced the first time I met her standing at my door.

We were still learning about the world around us through our many playdates of dress-up and our all-encompassing imaginations. It was a time of wonder, of traveling to magical lands as beautiful princesses that were always rescued just in the nick of time from a crumbling bridge, given way to the crocodiles surely awaiting our fall to the moat below or to the fire-breathing dragons that would be close to devouring us for a hot lunch. Fantasy was a large part of how we played, and it worked so well because we both thought the same way. Sometimes, though, I looked back on our shenanigans and wondered if we were close to real danger.

Thankfully, we had a great friend, imaginary though he was, named Zeus who always seemed to show up and save us. Zeus was a unicorn, or at least that's what we usually decided he was. Children's imagination has a lot of flexibility, so sometimes Zeus would change to be what we needed him to be for whatever game we were playing. On my birthday that year, Paige gave me a life-size stuffed unicorn and an *Everything That Glitters* makeup kit. I was so thankful I kept her birthday card and ensured it stayed by my side each night

I went to bed. It comforted me knowing it was there, tucked away in my nightstand drawer.

Each year, on the anniversary of her disappearance, I would reflect on the words she had written to me. This was the day. Friday, August 10. I paused, opening the card to see the familiar handwriting, drawing in a long, deep breath. "Dear Livvy, Thanks for being the sister I never had. I know we'll be friends forever, even when we have to rescue each other from the scary monsters in our magical, faraway land. Happy ninth birthday! Love, Paige."

Now, I was thirty-one, and I had never lost hope. I felt I was a considerable step closer to finding her as the new criminal investigator at the Bayfield Police Department. I couldn't shake the feeling she was still alive, although I was constantly reminded it was highly unlikely given that two decades had passed. She was telling me something in my dreams, but what? Over the years, I knew the only thing I wanted to do was keep my promise to find her after her case had gone cold with no investigative leads.

A part of me wanted to move far away to escape the torment I felt, but I vowed I would never leave until I could find out what happened to Paige. After receiving my Bachelor's degree in criminal justice, my main focus was to somehow get access to her case files. It was hard to believe nothing was ever found. Not one single lead? Something didn't feel right. The pain in my heart was still just as fresh as it was the day she went missing.

When was this dreadful feeling ever going to pass? Why hadn't she been found? What had happened to her? I somehow still felt responsible. Maybe if I had been there walking through the park with her, she would still be here. We had always felt safe in our neighborhood, but I knew I wasn't supposed to be out past dusk, so I declined her invitation to take a walk down to our favorite trail. The thought of her being kidnapped left a knot in the pit of my stomach.

We were both so innocent and didn't know bad people existed in the world back then, only that we shouldn't talk to strangers. It was a different world to me after her disappearance. A few months later, I was saddened to learn that Paige's parents were moving away. I never understood why they moved away so quickly. What if Paige came back? I had always wished I would hear her little taps on my front door again, but sadly, that day never came.

The weight of the tragedy must have been too much for her parents to bear, but I always felt it was strange that I never had the chance to say goodbye to them. One day, they just up and left. Did they blame me in some way? I was heartbroken when they decided to leave without saying a word, as I thought of Betty as a second mother. The police considered the case cold after three years to the day Paige went missing. It just didn't make sense. How could someone in a public park just disappear into thin air? What had happened to Paige in her final moments? Why had no one seen her in such a public area? After years of searching, I was still determined to find out.

2

The Bayfield Police Department was a well-kept building, but it always made me feel uncomfortable.

Of course, at the time, that could have just been my nerves getting the best of me since I was the rookie in the department and had much to prove. I hadn't even been working for a month when I decided that it was time to try to get Paige's file re-opened, but that had been anything but easy. That day, however, was going to be different. I had prepared for the anniversary by compiling my own case file and preparing to talk to Conrad Hudson, the chief of police and my personal mentor.

I had been lucky enough to get acquainted with many of the officers throughout my late childhood and adolescence, several being friends with my father. Conrad had taken me under his wing and was generally supportive, but he was also very pragmatic. If he didn't see the practical purpose of an assignment, he wasn't likely to permit it. For that reason, I felt the need to prepare for this day. It was imperative that I properly explained why I needed to pursue Paige's disappearance, and to that end, I had been consulting the friends I had made in the office so far.

As I settled down at my desk, a wave of nervousness blanketed me, hearing the telltale clicking of stilettos that signaled the approach of my friend Rebecca. Detective Rebecca Roan was the only person I knew at the PD who regularly wore high heels. She was also the first friend I'd made there that I hadn't already known. Her hazel eyes and curly brunette hair were almost as distinctive as her sense of style.

Rebecca walked over to my desk and looked down at the files before turning her attention to me. Her gaze was sharp and penetrating, and it never felt like I could hide anything from them. "So, this is your Paige file? There's not much here, Olivia." She frowned, looking concerned. "Are you sure you're ready to talk to the chief?"

I smiled at her. "Yeah, that's all that was documented about the disappearance in the public record." I looked down at the file, feeling bitter. "No one cared enough to make more out of the case." I opened the file, staring at the missing person poster inside. The picture they used of Paige was from our third-grade school picture day, and it didn't capture how I remembered her.

I remember talking to the policeman twenty-two years ago, but I can't remember his face at all. It was like looking at some concoction of vague authority. Every time I think back to it, I can't decide on his appearance, so my mind fills in the blanks, for some reason beyond me, and the officer becomes like a collage of different eyes and mouths. It is as though someone cut them out from magazines and pasted them over the canvas of my faded remembrance. His voice is never clear either; all that's apparent is that Paige is gone and I'm being asked where she is. I know I was scared and confused. I detest this memory.

I realized that I had been staring at the folder for a moment and snapped myself back into my present reality. "Terrible, isn't it?" I looked back toward Rebecca as she smiled at me sadly, her eyes still boring into me. As friendly as she was, I always felt like a rabbit looking at a hawk when I was near her. She always felt a bit intimidating to me, but I'm sure that trait served her well in her ten-year career as lead detective.

"Yeah, it is. I'm just worried it won't be enough." I shrugged, closing the file. "I'll just need to hope it is. Do we have anything going on this morning?"

I didn't want to talk more about this. As much as I appreciated Rebecca, she always seemed concerned when I brought up Paige. Something about her mannerisms told me that my goals with Paige's case made her uncomfortable, though I didn't know why. I didn't feel it was appropriate for me to ask either. I knew that she had her own issues to deal with, and given her experience at the station, it wasn't unreasonable to assume that the whole thing may have hit close to another case she had worked on. Knowing how painful that experience was, I would prefer to avoid dredging up any painful memories for anyone else.

"Yeah, we do. There's been a breakthrough in the Preston case, and we have a person of interest to bring in for questioning." That was big news. The Preston case was the first job I was assigned when I started at the police department. An eighty-five-year-old veteran named Walter Preston was found dead in his driveway. Forensics revealed that he died after being stabbed multiple times. His house had also been burglarized. Aside from my goals in re-opening Paige's investigation, this was the best news I could have hoped for, and I was eager to get justice for the poor man.

"Alright! Let's get going then. I just need to talk to Coop, and then we can go!" Cooper Harrison, or just "Coop," was a friend of my father, and he was also the attorney the police department kept on retainer. Thanks to my already existing relationship with him, I had his ear on most matters, which was helpful because he was probably one of the closest confidants of the chief. I had been consulting with Coop for the past two months, even before I had come to the station, trying to use him as an intermediary between me and Chief Hudson. As much as Conrad seemed to like me, I knew he still viewed me as a rookie and, therefore, wouldn't take much stock of my opinion on such an obscure cold case.

Rebecca nodded, rushing out of the room to retrieve the case file for our person of interest. I paused, waiting until the clicking of her heels fell silent. Assuming she was in the evidence room, I hurried through the large, sterile hallways overlooking the building's front courtyard, crossing the main campus of the police department that led to Cooper's office. It was hard to get used to the difference in scenery when you crossed into this outdated wing of the building of what the senior officers called the "old station." Suddenly sterile and overly clean environments gave way to an outdated and somewhat hospitable environment. A combination of grassy notes with a hint of underlying mustiness overwhelmed my senses, reminding me of the countless hours studying forensic science at the library. Gone were the linoleum and fluorescent lighting, replaced with wood and old incandescent bulbs still flickering in lamps. Something seemed oddly familiar about it from my childhood, but I didn't remember much from the time following Paige's disappearance.

Since starting at the PD, it became almost a daunting task to reminisce about my childhood since I came to realize that so much of my memory was tainted or incomplete. Faces never seemed to come to me, just like the policeman from that day all those years ago, and voices were muddled like I was listening with earmuffs. I couldn't remember the exact wordings people used in those days either. It was as though my mind was filled with vague impressions of a past that was only half lived. The rest of it was like I was within a dream, or sometimes a nightmare. I had considered seeing a psychotherapist to see if I could undergo hypnotherapy to regain clarity of that traumatic time. Still, Dad seemed to think it was a foolish plan, and I believed him.

I now stood in front of the heavy wooden door that marked Cooper Harrison's office. Aside from some older detectives, he was one of the only people who decided to stay back in this wing. Perhaps it was because of his archaic style, or maybe it was just that he didn't like being bothered, but I knew he wouldn't mind my company.

Opening the heavy door, I found myself surrounded by stale air that compounded the impression that I had in the outside hall. Cooper's office was filled with legal books and a collection of antiques, which added to the musty library-like atmosphere of the old wing.

The attorney appeared contrary to his position and tastes, instead striking anyone who passed by as a particularly casual family man. He was heavyset and just beginning to go bald. He also had a preference for business casual attire that made him exude a comfortable, if not somewhat tacky, air. As soon as I entered, the older man beamed up at me, crossing the room to envelop me in a hug. It didn't matter to him that I had seen him just several days before. What mattered was that he was seeing someone who was a friend. In a way, I truly appreciated his warmness and honesty. It certainly wasn't something you would typically find in a lawyer.

"Olivia! How are you doing?"

"Hanging in there, Coop. You know what day today is, right? I'm getting ready to talk to Chief Hudson. I was wondering if you could put in a good word for me before my meeting this afternoon." In some ways, I felt bad about using my connections for the sole purpose of accomplishing my goals. At the same time, though, considering my position, I knew he could get things moving in a way I just couldn't. Besides, he had made it abundantly clear that he was willing to help me however I needed. Just like everyone else, I got the impression that Coop didn't believe there was a fundamentally good reason for me to go after Paige, but still, he came to my aid and helped me move things along. As much as it infuriated me that the people around me didn't believe in my mission, I was always thankful that they seemed genuinely concerned despite not sharing my sense of duty.

Coop thumbed through the materials of my file, looking up at me with a pensive stare. "There's not very much here, Olivia. I'm sure you know that could make things difficult." He placed Paige's missing person poster on his desk and sifted through the years of notes I had gathered. An awkward silence filled the room as my anxious gaze fell on her angelic face. What happened to that little girl . . . my best friend . . . my sister? Coop turned to solemnly face me, sighing heavily. "Look, I'm not an officer. I can't tell the chief what to accept, and I don't have any authority, but he knows you're a good person, and I can vouch for that. I'll do what I can. Just don't expect miracles." I already knew it would be an uphill battle, so I wasn't discouraged.

"That's all I need, Coop. It's going to be a process of getting anyone to accept that this is a good idea, especially since I'm only going on a hunch. I just appreciate you going to bat for me at all."

The attorney shrugged and smiled. "It's the least I can do for you. You and your father have always been good friends to me. If there's one thing I don't want to be remembered for, it's not paying my debts." I nodded, though internally I didn't know what I had ever done for him. On the other hand, my father might have helped Coop out in some tough situations, but that wasn't anything I knew about. Ever since the disappearance of Paige, my father had been more and more distant. Once I was in high school and especially college, our relationship became cold and strained. Not that we were on bad terms; it's just that we didn't seem to see eye to eye anymore. Again, he had fallen into a restless and depressive state that he couldn't seem to claw his way out of. At times like this, I wondered who my father was to the people around me. Everyone seemed to think of him as a kind and respected man. And, of course, I loved him as well. I just wished I could have seen that warm and lighthearted side of him again.

My phone vibrated in my pocket, and I realized it had been a while since I left my office. I knew that Rebecca would be waiting for me and that it was most likely her who had texted me. I turned to hug Coop and thanked him before rushing out. I had a looming feeling that today would be long and difficult, and still, anxiety was mounting in my mind about the upcoming talk with Chief Hudson. I took a deep breath to collect my thoughts and stepped out into the sunshine, mentally preparing for the job ahead.

3

Just as I had assumed, the text was from Rebecca, who, at this point, was getting somewhat agitated that I had not been waiting in the car. I hurried to the lot, where an unmarked cruiser was waiting. There was no reason for us to raise any suspicion or alarm since we were just picking up a person of interest.

One of the first things I learned on the job as an investigator is that there are times when circumstances call for tact and other times when force is necessary. When looking for someone who may have been involved in a crime, it is best to let them think that you don't know as much as you do. As we climbed into the car, I was already formulating a basic plan for questioning in my head. Of course, I was also sure that Rebecca was doing the same thing, and as the more experienced investigator, I would defer to her better judgment. Eager to know what she was planning, I hastily blurted out, "So what info do we have on this guy? What's the plan?"

The detective kept her eyes on the road, with no indication of hearing my question, but instead gave the slightest gesture toward a file she had put on the dashboard. "Our man is named Jimmy Madden, twenty-eight years of age. We got a report that his neighbor saw him come home about an hour after the murder with stained clothes, looking distressed." I frowned, as there wasn't much to go on, but if Jimmy had anything to do with the murder, we needed to be careful in extracting information.

"I'm guessing we don't have a search warrant?"

Rebecca shook her head. I already knew the answer before I asked, but I felt it necessary to check everything. It would have been extremely difficult to obtain a warrant in such a short time, but it would probably be our best chance of getting any solid evidence. As we approached the man's home, I took a deep breath, knowing this would be a huge test of my skills.

I was having trouble focusing on the case at hand, knowing that I needed to give Paige's cold case the attention it deserved. Everything around me triggered half-remembered, half-imagined images of the past and the odd fragment of a sentence here, eyes staring from the murk there. They were less frequent than they used to be, but still, I occasionally had these episodes of unreality. I believe it was due to having such a traumatic event at such a young age. It's funny in a sort of cosmic way; you never know how something will affect you until later in life. I was devastated when Paige initially disappeared, but I never knew it would affect my psyche how I now know it did.

Back in college, these attacks would send me into a state of panic. Now, I was more at peace with them, realizing they were nothing but a symptom of my past. Still, though, they were disorienting, and ideally, I would have liked to step to the side and take a few deep breaths. That wasn't an option at the moment. Instead, I would need to push myself back into the right headspace for the task at hand and carry on. I looked over toward Rebecca's sharp features, and in the semi-nostalgic haze, I thought how much she must have looked like those officers I had seen when Paige disappeared. How much she must have looked like my teacher. How much everyone looked like someone from that terrible morning.

I knew this was simply a symptom of the face blindness that came with these episodes, but it made it no less disturbing. Once again, looking at Rebecca's unblinking eyes gave me the impression of a bird of prey or some predator gazing out into the forest looking for a victim. I shivered at the thought and redirected my attention back toward the road. At times like these, avoiding other people, especially faces, was my best option.

I was wondering what had triggered the episode. Of course, given the date, it could have just been the overwhelming stress, but looking at the surroundings, I realized we were nearing my childhood neighborhood. I could feel myself drifting as I looked out to the houses again. As much as I loved the thoughts of Paige and me playing here, it was impossible for me not to feel a sinister and overriding fear. My faulty ability to remember compounded this. I could see the trail leading to the beautiful lake, but now I could only think of walking.

A week after the disappearance, I remember that there was someone on the trail. I remember them approaching me and being scared of their sunken and beady eyes, but I don't remember what happened next, just being back in my home. There were so many memories like that, where they just ended abruptly. As I recalled this, my skin crawled, and I felt goose bumps developing along my shoulders and the nape of my neck. This was worse than the attacks had been in a while, and I felt sick. The knot in the pit of my stomach returned.

Though I didn't realize it, I must have been making some kind of odd noise, or perhaps I was shifting uncomfortably in my seat. Whatever the case, Rebecca pulled over to the side of the road and looked at me, her concern obvious on her face. "You're pale, Liv. Do you need a minute? Maybe some water?" Rebecca knew about my tendency toward these unfortunate episodes and was always extremely understanding. Weakly, I gave her a thumbs-up and said I was okay. It was a lie, but at times like this, I couldn't let myself be the reason we couldn't continue. If I was going to help people and bring justice to those who needed it, I had to act, and I couldn't hide behind what was ultimately my own issue.

The house we were looking for was only two streets down from where Paige and I had lived. It disgusted me to know that filth infested this place. Though, considering the abduction, perhaps it simply never left. Inside my heart, I felt a fire burn. I was angry; maybe it was for the wrong reasons, personal reasons, but if this man was guilty, I wanted him to rot.

Making sure everything was in order and double-checking our carry pieces, Rebecca and I walked up to the door. The house was in a state of obvious disrepair, and the doorbell didn't work. We shared a glance and a nod, and I sharply knocked on the door while Rebecca called out to whoever might be inside, "Bayfield PD, open up!" The two of us waited in silence. A few moments passed; my heart began racing wildly, ready to react to what was on the other side of the door . . . Then we heard it. Someone was whispering behind the door. I tightened my grip on the gun at my side. It wasn't unheard of for suspects in the area to open fire on officers, and I wouldn't let myself be a target.

After a few moments, the rustling subsided, and we heard a click on the other side of the door. It creaked open, revealing a small elderly woman. The older lady looked confused and adjusted her glasses, looking us up and down. "Oh, good morning. What can I do for you fine young ladies? Sorry for the wait. I was in the kitchen, and my hearing isn't the best, so I wasn't sure whether there was someone at the door or it was the television in the other room." I relaxed my grip on the gun and looked over at Rebecca. I hadn't been told there was anyone else living at this residence other than Jimmy, but by the look on her face, I didn't think she was aware of it either.

I made a note of her expression. As she looked at the old woman, I noted that the predatory gaze that was ever present on her features had melted away. Whenever she dealt with who she considered to be victims or witnesses, she put on a facade and acted incredibly kindhearted. Suddenly, Rebecca Roan, the detective, faded into obscurity, and into focus came a compassionate and harmless woman in her place. Truthfully, the detective's ability took me aback and made me less comfortable around her, but I knew how useful it must be.

Rebecca's voice was warm and friendly as she addressed the small woman. "We're sorry to bother you, ma'am. Is Jimmy at home?" Immediately, the woman's expression shifted. She looked discouraged and annoyed at the mention of the man we were looking for. Nonverbal cues are extremely important to notice as an investigator, and from the way she was acting, I knew something was going on between the two of them. Perhaps this was a relative, but whatever the case, she was not happy with him. "What has that boy gotten himself into now? Not only will he get a real job, but it feels like something happens every other week that makes someone angry at Jimmy. So tell me, what has he done to finally bring the police knocking on our door?"

This was a good sign for us. If she knew something about Jimmy's activity, she seemed like the type to share with the police willingly. Based on her reaction, it was evident that even if Jimmy Madden didn't have a lengthy police record, he was known for getting into a world of trouble. Still, I was getting ahead of myself. We couldn't be jumping to conclusions. "Ma'am, he may not have done anything. We don't know for sure; however, we need to talk to him about an event two weeks ago." Despite her apparent casualness, I could tell the older woman was getting more tense as we spoke.

She stepped aside and motioned for us to come in without saying anything. Only after we had stepped in through the doorway did she say, "Jimmy's room is in the back of the house to the left." I thanked her and walked back. Tension was building in the air, and I felt my hand drifting down toward my hip again. I quickly reminded myself that this wasn't a situation that I should bring my nervous tension into. Taking a deep breath, I tried to relax, and once again, Rebecca took the lead. I followed her to the unmarked door at the back of the house.

I was immediately struck by a smell that was something like rot mixed with a fungal stench. The air was exceedingly stale, and getting my first look into the room, I saw that it desperately needed to be cleaned. Jimmy Madden was on his bed, dead asleep, despite it being noon. Rebecca knocked on the side of the door loudly and cleared her throat to no avail. It took us both banging on the door and raising our voices to wake him up. Once he emerged from his inebriated state and started to stand, I thought it strange that he didn't seem surprised by our presence. Nor did he ask why we needed him to come with us. This was atypical for someone innocent. Usually, people would ask why we needed them or what this was about. A guilty man or a feeble-minded one who wasn't thinking of hiding his tracks wouldn't need to ask those questions because they already knew. Then again, most killers feel no remorse for their crimes. I couldn't help but think we might have the right guy.

The day continued productively, but I couldn't dismiss the thought of what was coming next.

Throughout our entire interrogation process of Jimmy Madden, I wasn't fully present, instead thinking of my meeting with the chief. Thankfully, my full attention wasn't entirely necessary, as Jimmy cracked under pressure like an egg. Equally, he was truly a disgusting man. He had become addicted to methamphetamine and wanted his next fix. It was then that he decided Preston, an acquaintance of his through a previous job, would be a good target. He had always found him to be easily manipulated and bullied and had ransacked the old man's house but wasn't expecting him to come in halfway through the burglary and attempt to fight back. This resulted in a brawl that led into the front driveway, where it escalated further, culminating in Jimmy stabbing Walter and running from the scene.

As I watched Detective Roan ask the hard questions and examine his testimony, it was apparent that he had spent no time planning what he could tell the police if he was tracked down. In a way, it was refreshing because he wasn't trying to escape justice. Still, in another light, it was infuriating, as he had taken someone else's life without considering how the consequences would affect him. After his confession, he dared to ask, "So, what happens to me now? Can I go home?" I couldn't look at such an evil man and not think back to Paige's disappearance. Every fiber of my being hoped she hadn't met a fate at the hands of one so insensitive and uncaring.

This was exactly why I needed to present my case and why we needed to reopen the case file of her disappearance and look into the matter. It was only based on my foggy memories and hunches, but I could not accept that she was simply gone, and if she was, I would find who did this to her. Either way, I wished to find her remains. Things needed to change, and as a cold case, nothing would happen. If I was going to make any progress toward resolving this, I would need Chief Hudson's approval.

I found myself standing outside the double doors, clearly labeled Conrad Hudson, Chief of Police. Conrad had a very large personality, and he was imposing. Even though I knew he thought of me in a positive light, it was always very intimidating to try to get anything from him. Opening the doors, I was immediately given the impression of how different Hudson's office was from Cooper's. Rather than being an old-fashioned or archaic type, Conrad was a judicious and especially pragmatic person. The inside of his office was more like a sterile office space, only scarcely decorated with awards and pictures of his family.

As I stepped into his office, Chief Hudson looked up at me from a packet of paperwork, one of many covering his desk. "Hello, Olivia. I'm glad you've stopped by. I heard that there was major progress on the Preston case. Excellent work on that." His voice was measured, even, and somewhat cold. This was just how he acted. It wasn't an indication that he was unhappy with you, but still, it made me feel uneasy in dealing with him. He was an exceedingly busy man, and I felt bad taking his time up, even if I was utterly assured that what I was bringing to him was important.

"Yes, sir, but I really must give most of the credit to Detective Roan. She has great instincts when it comes to dealing with suspects." Hudson absent-mindedly nodded his head, seemingly still absorbed in whatever he was reading on his desk. I wanted to give Rebecca every piece of praise that was due to her, and I certainly didn't want to take any of the credit she deserved. "I'm not sure if you know why I decided to request this meeting for today, but it's the anniversary of my best friend's disappearance when I was a child." The chief's eyes flicked up from his paperwork as he removed his glasses before turning his complete attention to me.

"We've talked before about your friend, Olivia, though I didn't know that today was the day that it all happened. I'm sorry for your loss. What can I do for you?" His decorum was appreciated, but this already was a bad start. *"I'm sorry for your loss."* That sentence did not leave a lot of wiggle room for other possibilities, at least in his perception. I had to go about this carefully. Now, at least, I had his undivided attention. He was not looking at anything else, which was completely uncharacteristic. I could count the number of times I had seen the chief paying attention to only one thing as opposed to multitasking on one hand and still having a couple of fingers remaining. What his reasons were, I didn't know, but he was listening.

I wasted no time taking my file out and placing it before him. "Sir, looking back at the public record for Paige's file, it doesn't look like our investigation was very thorough. If I could be so bold, I think that giving it another look could shed new evidence." I already knew that I was speaking too passionately. Chief Hudson wasn't the type to be swayed by an appeal to emotion, only an appeal to reason. When my eyes hesitantly met his, it verified what I feared. Conrad's face showed remorse and something akin to pity, but it lacked any sort of fascination that you would show a colleague who was presenting a practical idea.

Hudson sighed and put his reading glasses down, clasping his hands in front of him and then looking up at me. "Olivia, you are a great investigator. Even as a student, I could tell that, and I understand that this case was a big reason why you even wanted to get involved in police work. I have a lot of sympathy for you; however, I can't let you use the resources of the police department on something that I doubt will turn up any leads. Granted, we have more in our internal files than you have collected here, but it's not enough to have any working leads. I'm sorry, but I don't think Paige Phillips will ever be a closed case." There wasn't any anger in his voice, and I didn't get the impression that he was criticizing me. It was a simple matter of fact to him. There just wasn't enough to go on.

Even though a huge part of me knew this was how the meeting would go, I couldn't help but tear up. I was devastated; twenty-two years of my life had led up to my coming here. Two decades of effort, all in hopes of bringing closure to my childhood. "I understand, sir, but . . . if I could just be allowed to look at the files and work on my own time as a personal project. I have such a strong feeling that I could get to the bottom of this." I hadn't planned to say that, and none of this was part of my rehearsed plea. What was coming out of my mouth then was a desperate bargaining attempt. The chief sighed and shook his head. He stood from his desk and walked over to me, placing a hand on my shoulder. I think he could see that I was close to crying. I wiped my eyes, not wanting to appear weak in front of my mentor. This entire thing might have been a colossal mistake, but still, I had to stick to my ambitions.

"I don't like flattery, Olivia, but given the circumstances, I'm going to say it again: I see great things in your future as an investigator. That also means that I think it's best for you to move on. It's easy to get trapped in your past and start chasing ghosts. Back when I was starting, I had my own pet projects, things that never left my mind and kept me from sleeping at night. I think a lot of us bring those stories into work with us, at least at the start. But people who have a talent for this work need to move forward. We need to look to the future and to people who we can help now." His face showed the conviction he had in his words. I wished I could follow that advice. I wished I could just push my memories and the horror into a compartment and move on, but that wasn't an option for me. Part of me wanted to yell at him, but that would do no good, and he didn't deserve it. I swallowed hard and took a moment to compose myself before speaking.

"I see. Well, thank you for taking the time out of your schedule to talk to me, Chief. I won't bother you any longer." I tried to keep my voice as controlled as possible, but I knew that emotions still leaked into it, and it cracked randomly. Thankfully, Conrad wasn't the type to take advantage of weakness. Again, he patted my shoulder and returned to his desk, wishing me a good day. As I walked out of the office, I wondered what I would do moving forward. Approaching my desk, I slumped into my chair, throwing the file before me, opening it, and taking out all the documents I had gathered. For what felt like an eternity, I sat there looking at the missing person poster.

After sitting there, contemplating my next move in a state of shock, without warning, a fire lit inside of me. Suddenly, a sense of resentment boiled up. I had been going about this the wrong way. I did not need any approval to do my private investigation. If the police station wouldn't lend me their help or their files, that just meant I needed to take the lead. Where I would start or how I would do it, I didn't know, but what I did know was that I needed it to continue. On the surface, I understood and appreciated what the chief had said, but in reality, I was frustrated. How were we supposed to help anyone if we abandoned those in the past? It made us no better than those who ran from their toughest problems. What signal did this send, that you could beat justice if you could just secure the truth for long enough? I couldn't accept that.

As I sat there, becoming increasingly agitated and planning what to do next, I became aware that someone was walking toward my desk. Looking up, I saw Coop, an apologetic look plastered on his face. "Hey, I heard what happened. I'm sorry. I really did try to put in a good word for you. It's just, well, you know how Conrad is." I nodded my head. It wasn't Cooper's fault at all, but at the same time, I wasn't really in the mood to talk to him. I supposed I at least owed him that much, though, for trying to help. He came over and glanced at the file again. "So, Olivia. What's the plan now?"

5

The next few weeks of investigations were difficult. I was juggling the typical job cases, which was already quite stressful. Along with my pet project, I had nothing to go on and found myself visiting more and more places from my childhood. Overcoming the triggers of being back in my old neighborhood proved to be more than difficult while trying to ignore my nervous trepidation and the fear that crept in. I had also begun writing articles detailing what had happened to Paige and posting them to various forums online. I thought that perhaps by spreading the word of what had happened, I could gather support by throwing a wide net on the web. Maybe someone would know something or give me some kind of obscure lead.

On that day, I retraced my childhood steps on the path that led to the lake. I was met with the same phantom vision every time I came here. Walking down the path, and someone else walking toward me, grinning. Why did this continue to happen? I couldn't remember their face, their features, or anything about them. Aside from their smile, it was a blank void in my memory. Even all these years later, I was stunned by the beauty of the lake. I thought it was such a shame that a beautiful place like this had to be associated with such negative things in my mind.

There were better memories I had of this place as well, but they were tainted by what happened later. I recalled that Paige and I would come here and pretend to set sail on the lake, which we imagined as a sea. Depending on the day, a sea serpent might rear its head, or pirates would come looking for treasure. Whatever the case, we would get ourselves into trouble until our imaginary friend Zeus would sweep in heroically at the last minute. Sometimes, our outdoor play would get legitimately dangerous.

I could recall one summer day when we went swimming at the lake. We weren't supposed to be there unsupervised, but we felt empowered in our make-believe world and ventured down our favorite trail, daring each other to jump off the dock into the tranquil water that beckoned us. We were so engaged in our merriment and play, splashing and giggling, that we didn't notice we had drifted into deeper water and were further from the dock. We both started to panic, as we had exhausted much of our energy. Unbeknownst to us, we became entangled in an underwater current pushing us further and further out from the shoreline. We tried screaming for help, but that part of the lake didn't get many visitors since one had to hike down to its shore by trail. No one heard our cries for help.

To this day, I still don't know how we got out of that situation, as I could only recall that we screamed for Zeus, who we always believed came to our rescue. But as for how we got back to the shore, that part is lost to the fog of time. Thinking this way was beginning to put a smile on my face. Being back on this trail again, I couldn't help but think if this didn't turn up anything concrete, it might be good to revisit these places that haunted my psyche. I looked out onto the lake, watching the waves lap against the shore and enjoying the movements of the ducks as they played on its surface. Why was it that so many of my memories didn't make sense?

I was realizing now, especially over these past couple of weeks, that as I looked back into these places, things simply didn't add up. I knew that I had holes in my memory, but I didn't realize that it was so pronounced, so intense. What I thought was a record that stopped and started was more like a jumbled scrapbook of composite photographs. It was distressing to come to grips with how much you've lost without even knowing it. In truth, I was becoming worried that I might have early dementia. I had even scheduled a meeting with my doctor. All that I truly remembered and all that was really clear were the fantasies of those days and, of course, my friendship with Paige.

Above all, I didn't want those memories to fade and was terrified of what might happen if I didn't pursue this here and now. With the weight of that thought looming in my mind, I stared out at the lake. A sudden sharp noise shook me from my stupor and brought me crashing back to present reality. My phone was ringing. I took it from my pocket, expecting to see Rebecca calling me or maybe even my father. Instead, I noticed I was being called from a number I didn't recognize. I answered, but what met me on the other end caught me off guard.

A deep, smooth male voice immediately began to speak. "Hello, Olivia. I have information for you about the disappearance of Paige Phillips." I stood there with my mouth agape for about five seconds. In my mind, I cycled through all the possibilities of what this could be. Perhaps it was a prank call? No. No one I knew would be so cruel as to do that, and besides, no one I knew had a voice that sounded like this. Maybe it was someone replying to the post I had put online. I had never put my personal number in the articles, only the number for my desk at the police department. So that begged the question, who was this, and how did they get my phone number?

As cliche as the line was, I could think of nothing better to say than, "Who is this? How did you get this number?" I certainly wasn't worried about being polite. I wanted answers. The possibility did exist that someone had been following or stalking me. Of course, there was also the far-flung possibility that this was someone involved in Paige's disappearance. I hadn't thought I needed to keep this confidential, considering how long ago the abduction had taken place, but now the thought crossed my mind that my actions may have inadvertently put a target on my back.

The voice seemed unconcerned with my tone and replied very calmly. "My name is Luke. As to how I contacted you or who I am, aside from my name, that's not something I'd like to discuss over the phone. Would you be free to meet up? Of course, it can be in a public place, and as I said, I have information for you." My mind was spinning, and I had no clue what to say. The entire thing sounded dangerous; however, I could minimize risks if I could draw him out into public. At the same time, I was also an officer of the law. I could always arrest him or call for backup if things went south. Then again, I didn't know how much I wanted to involve the Police Department, considering they had technically forbidden me from continuing this investigation.

I thought momentarily before responding, resolute in my decision, knowing that I needed to move forward no matter the dangers. "Okay, Luke, you have a deal. I assume you know Harry's Bar? Let's meet there tomorrow at noon." Harry's wasn't far from the station, and it was in a heavily populated area. If something were to go wrong, people would see. Besides, I did have my service pistol. It's possible that I wasn't thinking rationally or even making the right decision, but that didn't matter to me. What mattered was that this could finally be a breakthrough in discovering what had happened to Paige.

I didn't know what awaited me; in truth, I was blindsided by how sudden this event was. Researching this Luke character made the most sense, but I had nothing to go on besides a phone number and a name, which was almost certainly a pseudonym. That aside, I didn't have much time for planning. One day simply didn't give me the luxury of preparation. Worse still, I didn't know how others in the department would react if they realized I was pursuing this case independently, especially if my work led me toward rendezvous with strangers. No, against my better judgment, I decided that I needed to handle this situation on my own.

The best thing I could do, and the only thing I could think of doing in this situation, was to make sure that I was alone and prepared to handle anything that could arise from our confrontation. I returned home and reviewed everything I collected about Paige's case. If this genuinely were going to be a meeting about evidence, I would need all of it. If it were a pretense to get to me alone, then it still wouldn't hurt to take along the compilation of paperwork I had tried to piece together for years surrounding Paige's disappearance; aside from that, I needed to focus on personal protection and security. Being a criminal investigator, I was well versed in self-defense, but I had also taken the liberty of getting myself tools for my civilian life. Ever since childhood, I was determined not to be a victim like Paige.

What I had laid out across my bed was everything I wanted to bring to the meeting tomorrow. Everything that I felt would protect me. I could wear a bulletproof vest underneath my outer layer of clothing and a larger holster to accommodate my full-sized pistol instead of my smaller sidearm that I usually carried as an investigator. Aside from that, I made sure I had my tactical glass breaker pen. My main goal was to avoid abduction. I left that night to scope out Harry's Bar and Grille. I needed to know every possible entrance and exit to the parking lot and be familiar with nearby places that could be used for shelter and areas that could be used for ambush. I needed to know everything there was to know about the meeting place.

I had chosen Harry's without overthinking it, with the probability of it being heavily populated. It was close to where I used to live, and perhaps subconsciously, I wanted to keep this meeting within that area, as if I could section off my pursuits from the rest of my life. This was a fool's errand. Seeing the restaurant immediately brought waves of nostalgia and regret. I was making all the wrong decisions for my mental health right now. It seemed that every place I went and directed my energy toward reminded me more and more of my past, bringing with it the panic and confusion that I usually spent so much time trying to avoid.

Harry's was a popular hangout with the locals. It had been around since the late '80s and was well known for its authentic New Orleans–inspired dishes and its central location to shops and sightseeing. I remembered going there on special occasions with Paige. I was a picky eater at the time. All I ever wanted was their Southern fried chicken tenders. Paige was always better. She would eat adventurously, and I would always crinkle my nose when I looked at her plate and say, "Eww. How can you eat that?" She always smiled and just said that there was more that tasted good that I hadn't learned about yet. She was always mature like that, but I loved that about her and enjoyed going there with her and her family. I never went back again after Paige disappeared.

Sitting in my car assessing the lot, I noticed an exit to the left, leading down a side street. It felt like someone was beckoning me there as I followed its path to a glistening lake with a large promenade surrounded by beautiful flowerbeds, ornamental shrubs, and native trees. My eyes followed the flakes of golden sunlight that made a series of soft rustlings as they touched the water. I couldn't tell you the reason why, but sitting there, I began to cry. My mind drifted back to my playdates with Paige, strolling hand in hand down our favorite trail to the water's edge. The sweet memory quickly faded with an unearthly feeling of dread. Something told me that there was trauma hidden in the murky depths of my memories that I hadn't yet confronted, but now was apparently not the time for me to see it yet.

I sat and thought I was trying to awaken some new memories as I tried to think of what had happened around Harry's. There were, of course, the memories of eating inside, but even those were somewhat disjointed. Why was there sometimes another place set at the table? I could almost swear that there was someone else eating with us, but I couldn't remember who they were or what they were eating. Suddenly, though, my blood ran cold. It was crystal clear, not a memory so much as a singular image, but with clarity that was astounding. I remember being with my father at this exact spot across from the restaurant as a child. I recall playing on the shoreline as he became preoccupied with a phone call, and something suddenly told me to focus on the water.

As I stared down at my reflection, Zeus majestically appeared to me, but not as I normally thought of him. Usually, when I thought of my imaginary friend, he was like a toy or a cartoon. In this image or memory, though, I saw a real horse with a horn—a white stallion, large, too, about the size of a draft horse. I knew this had to be a fabricated memory, but what trauma was hidden under such a fantastic image? Turning back to my steering wheel with a shuddering breath, I resolved that I might finally have some answers tomorrow.

Sleep had completely eluded me that night.

It didn't matter what I did; all I could do was toss and turn in my bed, so eventually, I gave up trying, instead focusing on what I would ask this stranger who went by Luke. By the time the sun had crept over the horizon, I had enough questions to fill a small journal. Even with yesterday's preparation, I felt scared and almost cornered by the possibilities of what was coming. I imagine it's a similar feeling to someone going to prison for life, except instead of living in fear each day of what they might encounter on the inside, I was coming toward the most dangerous of answers. The truth could give me closure, but it also threatened to throw me into a depression I doubted I could ever claw my way out of. Everything hinged on what he would tell me and whether it was true.

The morning came with a sense of dread and profound reflections on making myself look natural with the gear I was bringing. An oversized sweater that was adequately loose could conceal both the holster that would be mounted on my shoulder and the bulletproof vest, but I wouldn't be able to draw the gun in defense if things took a turn for the worse. Instead, I opted for an oversized flannel and a vest, making me look outdoorsy and maybe a little frumpy but certainly not abnormal or dangerous. I deliberately left my hair frizzy to complete the look, wanting to seem like I had been engaging in outdoor activity. Checking the mirror, I saw that the illusion was well crafted and smiled to myself. Ten times out of ten, I would rather look eccentric than be in danger.

As I climbed in the car and prepared to go, that same image of the unicorn in the water replayed repeatedly. In my memory, there were words, this time muffled. I couldn't make them out, but I knew they were in Paige's voice. Once again, though, I could not shake the feeling that someone else was present just outside of that frame of memory, just outside of my consciousness, looking there with both of us. The uncertainty chilled me, and I felt like I was facing great danger.

The parking lot was almost empty. Harry's generally got its dinner rush after five o'clock. Right now, it was too early for there to be too many bystanders; however, it was late enough that there would be cooks and hostesses starting their dinner shifts. To the left of Harry's was Martin's Drug Store, which would always have patronage, no matter the time of day.

Despite my worry, I felt I had chosen a good place for this meeting to occur. Now, all that was left to do was wait. As I waited, my eyes strayed past the restaurant toward the pathway leading to the lake. Time seemed to dilate and stretch as I looked, superimposing my memory back to a different era, back to my childhood home to the park's trail where Paige had disappeared. I doubted that anyone remembered Paige Phillips other than me. Though the world had changed in general, stranger danger had changed how children interacted with the world, turning the old, enchanted trails to explore into dark and suspicious places where strangers could be waiting.

I have no clue how long I sat there, or how long my mind danced with the long-forgotten possibilities of what had happened in my childhood or those new and disconcerting realities that came with the understanding of adulthood; however, when I tore my gaze away, feeling my obsession fading and my stupor coming to an end, I realized that the time for the meeting had arrived. Sure enough, as I gazed around the drab parking lot, there was a new and distinctly out-of-place sedan situated between me and the restaurant. It was black and unmarked to the point where there was no hood ornament or badge signifying its make or model; though a minor detail and technically legal, the obscureness of any identifying features made me uneasy.

Just then, my phone rang as I read "Unknown caller." I was sure I knew who was calling me as I picked it up and placed it against my temple, not sure what to say, listening for him to make the first move. The voice on the line was smooth and velvety, and it held mystery and promise that I could not yet understand but filled me with a mixture of trepidation and excitement. "I'm so happy you've decided to meet with me, Olivia. Would you prefer that we step into the restaurant or meet inside one of our cars? Perhaps you even wished for us to simply meet out in the open where anyone could hear us." The tone was mocking, but not in a way that held malice or hatred. It almost felt as though I was being teased by someone who cared. Involuntarily, I felt my face flush, knowing that I had overlooked the exact details of how exposed we would be if we were just standing outside in a parking lot. I wouldn't say I liked the idea of inviting him into my vehicle, nor going into his, and so, it seemed that I was about to go to lunch with the man I knew nothing about.

"When you put it that way, I guess going into the restaurant is fine."

While still deep and level, there was the smallest element of delight in the voice's response on the phone. "Excellent. Then we'll call it a date." I didn't know whether he was mocking me or trying to make a joke, but a slight chill ran down my spine, and I found myself reaching unconsciously for the pistol at my side, gripping it nervously. I took a few deep breaths and prepared myself to head in. "I'll go in first. You wait a minute, or however long it takes, to gather your thoughts for what you want to ask me, and then just come to my table. Don't worry, I'll ensure the waitress holds off on bringing drinks until you're in." I was starting to get annoyed. Whoever this man was, he clearly felt like he had all the power here, and he was also too familiar for my liking.

Part of me wanted to watch the figure leave the sedan and head into the restaurant, but something kept me from doing so. The part of my brain that was still little Olivia, the same part where boogeymen still lived and where awful things crawled in dark corners . . . that piece of me kept me from looking. I was almost sure that I would see something abnormal slinking from that black car, so abnormal that I couldn't reconcile it with how I forced myself to view the world. I tried to dismiss the bizarre image that came to mind of the police officer from that fateful day and that pasted-on smile, such as one would see in a magazine, haphazardly smacked onto his nonexistent features.

I sat there for a long time with my face averted, making sure that I wouldn't see anything. My mind was a muddled mess. I knew, however, that I could not simply sit here, and so, taking deep breaths until I regained some degree of control over my emotions, I resolved to go into the lion's den. I walked from my car toward the restaurant, now transfigured from a nostalgic piece of my past to an alarming sense of terror. With each step, my anticipation of what I would meet inside grew. Suddenly, I was startled by the realization that I had begun to personify this man I had not yet met into not only my friend's captor but also the source of all of my fears and trauma. Whether this was simply a flawed coping mechanism or an extremely unhealthy stretch of the imagination brought on by my independent nature, I could not say.

Walking into a family restaurant so early in the day provides a sense of surreality. It's open, it's functioning, but there is no one there. For a moment, I felt as though I was in a subliminal space, though the feeling quickly subsided as a hostess came up and asked with a smile on her face if I was the woman that the "gentleman in black" was waiting for. I swallowed past a sudden tightening in my throat and nodded. I was led into the dining room, which was empty except for one dimly lit booth in the far corner.

Sitting at the table was a man in a black suit. I would estimate he was perhaps a few years older than me. Rather than anything I was expecting, my first impression of him was that he was easy on the eyes. He had gaunt, sharp features and sandy blonde hair swept to the side. He exuded a sense of formality and politeness, and something about his gaze, which at the moment was directed out the window, was penetrating in its intensity. It didn't bear the same predatory nature as Rebecca's, though, instead holding within it a depth of wisdom that looked beyond his apparent age. It must have only been a moment that I stood there looking before he turned to me, a smile blooming across his features. Just like his eyes, the smile held an intensity that was entirely pleasant and unthreatening. It was difficult for me to understand what I was seeing in the depths of his expression, but there was something deeply comforting about him. That in itself, however, made me uncomfortable, as though there was a spell cast over me.

The man gestured toward the other side of the booth, his smile not diminishing. "Olivia, please take a seat. I've been waiting, but not too long. As I promised, I waited for you to order drinks." His voice was even deeper off the phone, and something to its tone evoked a pang of nostalgia within me. I froze as my gaze fixated on him. I didn't remember this man, yet something about him was so characteristic of an experience in my childhood. This left few options, and none of them were pleasant. Hesitantly, I edged close and sat down, my right hand hovering over the spot on my vest where I knew the .45 caliber pistol was waiting should something go terribly wrong.

As I settled into the seat, I looked into the stranger's green eyes, searching for motivation and meaning. "Trust is a two-way street. So far, you've done nothing to gain mine and used every advantage you have to get me here. I think I should ask a question first; depending on how you answer, things will either get better or worse. How do you know my name?"

His lips formed a half-hearted smile as he shrugged. "Well, to begin with, Olivia, your name is public record; you are an officer of the law, after all. As for why I'd go through the trouble of finding that out, though, well, it's my job." I cocked an eyebrow, not liking that answer. I think he picked up on that, as he continued, "I mean, it's my job to know things. You see, I'm an investigator, not like you though. I don't work for the police department. I'm a private investigator and have my own interests, just as I'm sure you do." He lowered his gaze, staring at me with a knowing look through his eyebrows.

My grip tightened. Even though something about his presence was comforting, everything he was saying was setting off alarm bells for me. My gut was telling me that this man, "Luke," as he called himself, was nothing but danger. "Well, Luke, you must be one hell of a detective to have gotten my private phone number and to know what I'm working on, even when the department doesn't." His smile disappeared into a frown. It wasn't a mocking gesture; instead, he seemed genuinely hurt by my insinuation.

"I realize that this isn't the ideal way that we could have met, and honestly, I had pictured this differently as well, but there's a time for waiting and a time for action, and that time is now." He lifted a briefcase next to him, unclasping it on the table and opening it, revealing a large assortment of paper files. "Olivia, this is everything I've gathered. I want to help you find Paige Phillips."

7

Luke's file, or briefcase of files, as it were, was massive. Contained inside were various pieces of information from missing person cases, murders, people of interest, cult activity, and other even stranger occurrences in the area dating back through the past twenty years. Even just slightly digging into it, I was completely overwhelmed by how much information was there and how little of it seemed to pertain to my case. I looked up at him questioningly. Surely he must have known how far from helpful any of this would be. Perhaps he was trying to taunt me? When I looked up to meet his eyes, expecting the telltale signs of mockery in his features, I was surprised to see him serious and sober, the most intense he had looked since I'd walked in. "What do you make of these?"

I didn't know where to start or how even to begin to address it. I began to dig through the seemingly unrelated files and incident reports and felt a growing sense of unease with every passing moment. Missing person after missing person after missing person. There must have been hundreds of records of them just in one section seemingly dedicated to these missing person's reports inside this case. As I looked up at him, it dawned on me that he must have been able to tell on my face just how concerned and confused I was. "You've never seen these reports before, have you?" he asked. I immediately turned the papers over as our waitress made her way to our table, looking inquisitively between the two of us as she silently poured us a cup of coffee, and then just as quickly left. Luke's eyes met mine as he took a long sip; though his expression was seemingly placid, there was a certain tremble to his voice that told me there was fear behind it in the way he was regarding the information.

I shook my head, stunned, taking out more of the flyers and spreading them around. An overwhelming majority were children, though others were younger adult women, and some younger men dotted here and there, as well as the occasional older person. "What is this? What are you trying to tell me? Are you trying to say that I should forget about Paige because other people have disappeared? Aside from that, I don't know about any of these cases. I don't know if this is a sick joke, but you'd better start answering some questions." I glared at him furiously. I was used to people trying to persuade me, but I wasn't used to this psychological warfare against my efforts.

Luke's face contorted into something between a mixture of pity and distaste.

"Olivia, you should know by now that the police department keeps many records you can't access. What I'm showing you here isn't hoax material that I've made, and I'm not taunting you either. I'm trying to drive home a point. This is the material that you can get from unsealing a small fraction of Bayfield's cold case files. Do you know how much above the national average the rate of disappearances of minors is in this town? People are abducted at twenty times the national average here, Olivia." I looked over the sheets again, this time paying more attention to the details. They all had proper watermarks; some were even labeled with tamper-proof ink. Undeniably, these were from our police records, but I had never seen them, nor was I aware of any of them. Worse still, as I looked through, I realized that several of these abductions were recent.

My mind was reeling, and my head was spinning. I knew a terrible realization was dawning on the edge of my consciousness, but I refused to look it in the face. It was too awful to quantify in words what I was being shown, what my mind knew must be the true purpose in showing this to me, so instead of simply accepting it, I numbly asked, "What exactly are you trying to tell me, Luke?" My hands were a numb bundle of pins and needles. I waited for the response. My heart thudded in my chest as I went over those same childhood memories in my mind again and again. Except this time, I couldn't fend off the thoughts of all the other children walking along the streets, suddenly gone from the picture.

All I could think of was that figure without a face, without a defined body. The figure that approached me near the lake, smiling. That fake smile that my mind had to fill in, that same smile that my mind placed on the police officers. I didn't know whether I was panicking or going insane or whether my condition was acting up. I didn't know what was happening inside my head or what truth awaited me, but it didn't matter at this point. An awkward silence filled the air, though I knew it must have only been a moment that felt like an eternity, waiting to confirm the deepest fears of my nightmares.

As I sat there, folding in on myself and collapsing, I felt a reassuring grip on my right shoulder. Looking up, I saw that Luke had reached across the table and grabbed me. It wasn't an aggressive gesture at all, but rather the same way a man would grab a sister or a friend, as if scared I would faint, his eyes full of compassion and empathy. The way his mouth furrowed told me that he was worried about what was happening in my mind. I didn't know this man. I didn't know where he came from or who he was, and to add to that list of unknowns, I didn't know why he seemed to care. Slowly and with great emphasis, he began to speak, and now, he spoke at length.

"Olivia, I do not believe that Paige Phillips simply disappeared. I believe that she was abducted, the same as all these other people. I also believe there is a trail to discover what happened to her and where she is. In my research, I found you. You are the only link I could find who hasn't given up on Paige, and I want to help you. I know this will sound strange, and it won't make sense right now, but you need to believe me when I say that the one to find her must be you. It can't be me, but I can give you information and leads to get you on the right track and support you." He was right. I didn't understand what he meant by that.

Why couldn't it be him? Certainly, it seemed that his ability to get information was greater than my own. Other than my personal relation to Paige as a child, there was nothing that made me special. Still, though, there was something about the resonance of his words, the way he delivered them. Looking into his eyes, I knew instinctively, with every fiber of my being, not just as an investigator but as a person, that he was telling me the truth. I was also sure that there were things he was leaving out. It didn't take an expert to see that this mysterious stranger was a secretive sword, but rather than the villain I had expected to meet, I believed that he was, at the very least, a force for good.

Trying to digest this information was interesting. Hearing those words I had wanted to hear for so long was a rush of exhilaration—that someone finally believed what I had been saying, that someone else thought Paige was still out there. At the same time, the entire situation seemed completely and utterly insane, and I didn't know how to process the information I was being given logically. I still didn't even know how Luke had found me, and a part of me felt like I had stepped into some *Twilight Zone* episode.

As much as he said he was a private investigator, I still had no clue who this Luke person even was, and at this point, I didn't know if I wanted to question his story. There was so much appealing to the fantasy and the idea that what was, in essence, a guardian angel had simply appeared to help me on my quest. I wanted to ignore the obvious logical strangeness of the situation, and so, against any better judgment, at least at that moment, I did. Of course, later would come the research on who this man was, and later it would come to the confrontation of his real motives, but right now, I needed to believe he was here to help. "What can I do to get started?"

Luke beamed at me, apparently very happy and satisfied that I was listening to him and not storming off. He dug deeper and deeper into the briefcase, pulling out a small manila envelope. His soft green eyes focused on mine as he slowly opened the envelope and pulled out a handwritten note. He passed it across the table to me. Looking at it closer gave no clue as to what exactly it was, as it was just a collection of numbers and letters. He looked at me expectantly for a few moments, hoping that I would make sense of it, but when it became evident that I didn't know what I was looking at, his face softened a little, and he went on to explain, "I guess you never were into treasure hunting as a child. Those are coordinates. I'm sorry that I can't just give you destinations and street addresses, but some of the places you're going to need to go aren't marked by buildings, and the others are too sensitive for people to know where you're going." Something about the way he said that made me feel very uncomfortable.

I had no clue what exactly he meant by the idea that a location would be too sensitive to simply give it to me in a handwritten form. To me, at best, that sounded paranoid. At worst, it sounded like a way to try to give information that would lead someone into danger, but still, I took the envelope. He nodded his head anxiously as he continued, "Those coordinates right at the top will be the most important thing for you to visit, so it's where you should go first. I know that this will make me sound even more suspicious to you, but I have to warn you that you really shouldn't let anyone know where you're going."

I cocked an eyebrow. "Uh, why exactly would I not want people to know where I'm going?" It only had taken that one sentence to somewhat snap me back into my normal mental faculties and critical thinking. That was such a strange and frankly dangerous thing to ask of me. Immediately, I was back on my guard. Luke could also tell and quickly threw up his hands in a kind-hearted gesture. Where exactly was he sending me? What was happening here? I knew it couldn't be mentally healthy, but I was going back and forth from emotional extremes of happiness, hope, and absolute terror. Then, a thought pierced my mind: how did he find me? I still didn't know, but he knew about Paige and my goals to find her, and now he was trying to get me to go somewhere isolated alone. I had initially worried that perhaps this man was the one who had abducted Paige, but seeing him now,

I knew he was far too young to be the culprit; however, the possibility of him being an associate was still fresh in my mind.

Luke was obviously sharp. He leaned forward immediately, cleverly sensing my apprehensiveness, and was quick to alleviate my fears. "Listen, I know what you're thinking right now. You're thinking, oh, he's trying to get me alone. Oh, he's trying to hurt me. That couldn't be further from the truth. Look again through these files. This is still happening, and you might not have noticed that some of the people who have gone missing in these past twenty-five years are police! I need you to be secretive because I think someone is watching you."

It had been two days since I met the man who called himself
Luke.

I never learned what he tried to pass off as a last name.
The strange rantings he had gone on that day were enough
to send me reeling, but I was left with that manila envelope.
Despite how promising it had all seemed at first, I had the
impression that whoever he was, he was either dangerous
or very diluted. He seemed to think there was a conspiracy
surrounding missing people in the area. With no help from
the police department on re-opening Paige's cold case or a
direction to take on any leads, I kept the envelope he had
given me. Despite all the strangeness I encountered that day,
I was determined to figure out where it led.

The warnings of this stranger had not discouraged me, and
I was not about to fall victim to being a lone person going

about this. I may have been investigating in my own personal capacity and yearning for my freedom, but that didn't mean I was foolish. With that thought in mind, I walked into the police department. Perhaps I couldn't rely on the resources of detectives. For example, I couldn't go to Roan, but there were plenty of other people who could help, and I happened to know that there was one man in the department who wasn't a cop who would have the resources and expertise I needed.

With that in mind, I confidently strolled past my desk and into the ever-watchful gaze of detective Rebecca Roan. I intended to continue past her, but she stood up, blocking my path. "Hey, Liv, you've been a hard person to reach this past week. Did you know that?" There was an edge in her voice. It wasn't exactly anger or annoyance, but there was something underneath it that she was trying to say other than that. I simply wasn't as available as usual. Her gaze was always penetrating, but now I felt as though that hawk-like stare fixed on me the same way it would a criminal, and I felt a chill creep up my spine.

What was this conversation that we were about to have, and why was she looking at me like that? "I just want you to know, Liv, that if you ever need any help with things, I'm here for you. Please don't hesitate to contact me." She smiled then, but again, it didn't match her eyes. The only way I could adequately describe the uncanniness of the expression would be to compare it to plastic. The discrepancy between what she was saying and her body language was evident, and I didn't know what to make of it. It made me deeply uncomfortable, and suddenly, in the back of my mind, I remembered those words from Luke: that someone was watching. Of course, he hadn't been talking about Rebecca, and this was my own paranoia acting out, although her behavior was strange.

I had to make sure that how I presented myself was normal. Something deep within me told me that if I showed that there was something wrong, the situation would get worse, so I channeled everything into conjuring up a composed, apologetic smile, the kind that showed what kind of an absent-minded and harmless person I was. Right now, I needed to project that persona of myself, of how I knew she saw me as much as I could. There was no intellectual reason for it. After all, this was a normal enough conversation, but something deeper told me that it was important, and again, through my head danced the images of those people I couldn't remember and those features that would stare at me in my dreams. "Sorry, Rebecca, I've just been really tired recently. I put so much effort into getting that case together to show to the chief, but I guess it just took the wind out of my sails when he turned me down."

Rebecca continued to stare at me carefully. I didn't know what she was looking for, but I knew that even under normal circumstances, I would feel uncomfortable with the direction of the conversation. What was she trying to hide from me? What was happening here? I felt like all I did recently was ask questions and slip further and further into this state of uncanniness, but maybe the man had been right. Maybe things weren't as they seemed around me, and perhaps I needed to be more on guard.

After what must have been thirty seconds of this sustained stare down, Rebecca sighed, her smile becoming sad as she looked up at me. "So, you really did forget, didn't you?" I forgot what? What was she talking about? Suddenly, like a bolt of lightning, it hit me, and embarrassment flushed throughout every corner of my face. Today was Rebecca's birthday. In all that had happened in the last twenty-four hours, I had completely forgotten, and now she was standing in front of me, probably waiting for me to wish her a happy birthday like a normal person.

My expression alone told her of my absent-mindedness.

"Oh no, Rebecca, I'm so sorry! Of course, happy birthday!"

Now, her smile became much more genuine. "You do remember! I'll be real with you, Olivia; I was kind of worried and sad there, especially since you're the only one I made birthday plans with." I couldn't believe what a paranoid nutcase I had been. I was actually considering my friend as though she was a potential enemy. Seriously, what was I thinking? I needed to reevaluate things. I was getting lost in this odd fantasy, and as much as I needed to go and find out what had happened to Paige, I couldn't let it dominate my life like I was. I think it was then that I realized that what I was doing might not be very healthy. My mind drifted back to Luke sitting there with that massive case of files, so obsessed with the past and all the disappearances in the area. I had slowly let Paige's disappearance control the direction of my life over the last twenty-two years, wanting to stop at nothing to find my friend. Paige deserved justice, but I couldn't let myself get so wrapped up in all this. I shook my head. This was good. I needed this to ground myself right now.

I laughed and brought Rebecca in for a hug afterward, tilting my head and giving her a warmhearted smile. "Of course, I remember our plans, Rebecca. Don't worry. I just need to go drop off an envelope with Coop, and then you and I will head out for a nice lunch and some drinks." This was the only kind of normalcy that generally dominated my life, sometimes after a long day on a case. I had stepped away from it these past few weeks. I had never known how damaging it could be to my psyche, traumatized as I was, to leave it behind. I made a small vow to myself then that I would not abandon Paige. I would not stop my pursuit. But I couldn't keep going the way I was now that this mystery man who called himself Luke had appeared. What obsession did he have with those past cold cases? Was it a warning? All I knew was that I did not want to become like that. Strangely, I supposed I had a lot to thank him for. I still didn't know what these leads would turn up, but it was time to get to the bottom of it. Coop would help me, and I headed toward his office to give him the letter.

I hadn't been wrong in my assumption. The second I entered Coop's office, he greeted me with the same usual hug and warmness I would expect, asking and listening to my stories about the past few weeks. Of course, I neglected to tell him what I had been doing regarding Paige's case and instead focused on work and life, even though I had to add slight embellishments in some places to keep what I was doing secret. "You're always so busy, Olivia. Honestly, I think it would make your father sick if he knew you always worked yourself into the ground. It would help if you found an opportunity to relax more. Besides, there's so much that you could be doing and having fun with. You're still in the prime of your life." As usual, speaking with Coop was a lot like talking to an older relative who only wanted to see the best for you, and in many ways, that was comforting, if not slightly annoying. The mention of my father, though, did make me feel uneasy.

I'm sure that just about anything I did would make my father worry. He was just a nervous person at this point. I didn't like thinking about how broken he was these days, and as much as it might sound awful to say, I tried to limit my exposure to him as though his deep depression was contagious. However, this proved difficult in everyday life, as he clung to me like I was still a child. I often came home from work to see multiple missed calls. He always wanted to see what I was doing and how I was doing. It would be sweet if it wasn't tinged with this strange sadness that was so characteristic of his actions. I think he was afraid of losing me like he had Mom, but still, as an adult, I needed freedom and had grown distant.

Pushing the thought from my mind, I took the envelope from my purse and handed it over to the seasoned attorney.

"Hey, I'm sorry to bother you with this Coop, and I promise I mainly came here to catch up, but I've got a bit of a personal project that I was hoping you could help out with."

The old man's eyes lit up. Just like when I needed advice in dealing with Conrad, he was always happy to assist wherever he could. He happily reached out his hand and grabbed the envelope, looking at it with a slightly amused face. "Well, heck, Olivia, I'm happy to help wherever I can, but what exactly is this? These look like coordinates with latitude and longitude. What are you doing here? Are you on some sort of scavenger hunt?" Immediately, he began to copy down the coordinates.

"Well, it's something like that. I really just need to start with the one right on top. Apparently, it's all in sequence." Cooper nodded, obviously amused by what I was saying and what he was seeing. He got that dreamy look in his eyes that told me it was striking a chord of nostalgia for him.

"You know, when I was about your age, we'd do stuff like this too! Either we'd be in scouts, or we'd be, you know, on the lookout for exotic places to head to, and sometimes we'd find little rhinestones or treasures of some sort. I'll tell you what, it made me feel like a little adventurer. Those were the good ole days!" Coop continued on for a while, talking about his old adventures, as I sat there and nodded. I knew he would be able to get to the bottom of where that was, but I also knew it would probably take him a while. He wouldn't just give me the exact place. If that's all I wanted, I could have used the computer. Now, Coop would do some research and give me a bona fide report of all the information I could want on whatever this place was. I told him I would leave it to him, that I trusted him, and would come back for the information before heading home for the day.

I left to go celebrate with Rebecca. Little did I know that when I returned to the office, I would be met by Coop waiting at my desk. He had a look in his eyes I had never seen before. There was no warmth to him, and there was nothing except for one piece of advice as he handed the note back to me. "I don't know what you're playing at, Olivia, but you better quit while you're ahead. Some things in the past should be left there. Now, you should remember that and take it to heart. I don't know where you got that, but you best destroy it or just forget about it, okay?" Before I could answer, he turned away and laughed, leaving Rebecca to look at me, surprised and confused and leaving me even more intrigued than before.

9

Without Coop's help, I didn't know what I would be heading into, so I attempted to look up the coordinates on the computer.

Apparently, it led to a vast amount of land one state away. Not that far, though, only about a five-hour drive. However, when I saw where exactly this land was located, my blood ran cold. It's not as though anything was threatening about the location, but anytime a phantom from your past comes rearing its head, even if it isn't unpleasant, you find yourself shocked. The coordinates led to a place in Gainesville, Georgia. While I had nothing against Gainesville, it felt strange, putting an unpleasant taste in my mouth, knowing I had to go back to my old childhood stomping ground. But what did Gainesville have to do with Paige's disappearance? I had met her only after my father and I moved to Bayfield. I couldn't help but wonder if I was being set up.

Still, though, I was completely dumbfounded. There was nothing normal about Coop's reaction. Was he trying to say that I shouldn't go digging back into my past with my mother? Perhaps he thought I was trying to open old wounds or pushing myself too hard, but that probably would have evoked something close to sympathy from the old man, not outright hostility. In the next several days, he wouldn't even look at me. I came offering to take him to lunch, and he showed me out of his office without so much as talking to me. None of it was right, and as much as I had said that I would keep myself grounded, I again felt the strangeness and pull of the paranoia. Thinking back to Luke's sorrowful eyes, I thought perhaps there really was something to worry about. Whatever the case was, I wouldn't delve into it here, yet I still was as resolved as ever to continue my search for Paige.

With these thoughts swirling in my mind, the impulse to go to Gainesville that weekend was instinctive. Once again, I decided that taking my more heavily armored approach would be prudent, and so, in the same way I went to meet Luke, I stepped out on Saturday morning and loaded up the car for the trip. I had no expectations. I was hoping this would lead to something interesting or helpful, but at this point, I was entangled in my head with the distaste for what I perceived to be an insane man's ruse. I was prepared for the extremes of this, either being nothing whatsoever or the terrifying alternative.

The drive itself was exceedingly pleasant. Fall was subtly creeping into Florida, but crossing over into Georgia gave me a more unmistakable sense of the shifting of seasons. I enjoyed looking at nature at this time of year. As I was in no rush, I decided to take a more scenic route and was glad for the decision. Five hours in a car isn't exactly the toughest or most strenuous of journeys, but it is still tiring.

Entering Gainesville invited a flood of memories. Not all of them were straightforward. At one point, I might pass an abandoned parking lot, and a flash of a drug store that used to be there would come into my head. Mostly, though, my thoughts involved family, not Dad so much, though he was certainly there. My thoughts shifted to my mom and remembering her cooing after me as I went about my business as a small child. "Oh, Livvy, dear, come here." That was her name for me, Livvy. It made me feel warm inside to remember her voice, even as muddled as it was over the years.

There were other emotions as I went down those age-old roads, feelings I hadn't been expecting while revisiting the neighborhood of my childhood home. Maybe it would be an overriding positive experience after all, despite this being where my mother had died. It was also where I had been born, where I lived with Mom, where me and my dad spent our time. But why did an immoral sense of wrongness strike me at odd intervals? It was like a psychological stench, a robot that clung to the surroundings and made me feel violated. On more than one occasion on the trip, I felt the need to roll up the windows, turn on the air conditioning, and play music simply to cleanse myself.

I thought to myself about what I was feeling and attributed my discomfort to feelings about my mother's passing, though

I never consciously thought that they affected me this deeply. In my head, I always assumed that I was somewhat at peace with what had happened. Perhaps I had simply been too optimistic, but if it was true that I carried trauma about this part of my life, then I supposed it was a blessing in disguise that I had come here. Perhaps I could confront those feelings and attempt to move forward. Who knows what other parts of my life were hooked into that negativity and where I would see improvements if I could manage to move past it.

These thoughts danced in my head while I was in one of my usual introspective trances, until I started to realize something. As I got closer to my destination, I recognized more and more landmarks. I was not simply passing through a piece of Gainesville that I was somewhat familiar with; rather, I was traveling deeper and deeper into the territory of my formative years. The uncomfortable sensations I was experiencing doubled and then tripled until I found that I wanted to retreat into the shell of my psyche. This, however, was impossible as I continued to get closer and closer. A terrible realization was dawning on me, but it was confirmed too late for me to process it in full.

As the GPS alerted me that I had arrived at my destination, I looked up to confirm what I already knew in the pit of my stomach. Though I had never seen this home before, neglected and abandoned as it was, some part of my brain and heart knew that, in fact, I did know it. That at some far-flung point in time, I had been there. I felt like I had stepped into one of my dreams or nightmares and wished to stay in the car, but some strange force pulled me from my seat. As I walked up to the overgrown ivy-ridden gables of the large Victorian-style home, I tried to place where it had fit into my childhood, where I had seen it before, but to no avail. Certainly, I had never lived here, and none of my friends had either. So here it sat in front of me like some bloated tumor on my memory and psyche.

Stranger still than the nature of the house, in my mind, was its condition. Though it was obviously dilapidated and clearly abandoned, there was no particleboard covering the windows and no bolts covering the doors. In fact, as I walked up to the porch, which was caving in on itself in several places, and made my way to the door, testing the handle, I found that the place was unlocked.

Suddenly, it opened with a slow creak.

Without light inside, the building's dark halls sprawled before me, almost ancient, vast, and labyrinthine. Even though the house was not very large, I felt like a small child as I stood in the doorway looking into the gulfs of the house. This effect lived only in my head. I knew because, in reality, I was simply standing on an old porch looking into an old home that hadn't had an owner in maybe two decades. There was no mystique or mystery about what I was seeing; there was nothing supernatural or strange about it, but the illusion persisted, and I stood there frightened.

Deep down, I knew, or at least felt that I knew, that if I took a step inside, there would be no going back, but going back to what? I had no idea, but this discovery had a sense of finality, and the trepidation that plagued me was threatening to overwhelm my senses. A question repeated again and again like a bell tolling in my head, "Do you really want to know what's in there? Do you really want to know why you were sent here?" So I sat there, shivering like a leaf, stunned into inaction by some flight-or-fight response that reached up from my soul in response to a danger my mind and body didn't recognize.

How long I stood like that, staring into the inky darkness of the old, abandoned haunt, I do not know, but eventually, something changed. It was not a logical thought that spurred me into action. No reasoning or psyching myself up could get me through that threshold, but rather, it was a rogue memory, another image that floated into my consciousness of Zeus staring at me from the water. It was funny in a strange way; again came what felt like a tangible memory of something I knew I had simply daydreamed all those years ago.

But still, the image of the old unicorn filled me profoundly with courage and hope, a feeling I couldn't dismiss, as though something was watching over me. Just like all those times I played with Paige as a child and he had rescued us in our fantasies, I suddenly knew that things would be okay, and as I thought that, I remembered Paige's words from when we played down by the lake. "Come on, Livvy, we can't find any treasure if you don't keep going!" I smiled and stepped into the house.

10

My instincts had been right as I stepped through the threshold and looked around, my eyes adjusting to the dim lighting.

I felt an absolute horror creep through my veins and into my extremities. My fingers tingled, my face flushed, pins and needles ran up and down my back, and I felt like I would vomit. Memories hit me like a freight train. They were disconnected and disjointed, and they came with this real physical sense of discomfort and pain that I didn't understand, but instinctively, they jumped to mind. I had been here. So had my father. I was here with other people too. I couldn't make out faces, but I remembered yelling. I remembered laughing. I remembered people moving through the hallways hurriedly, lots of them too.

Maybe something like a house party? But I had been here, and I remembered it being scary. A friend of mine who studied human psychology back in college had once told me that certain places from our past can hide from us in our heads and, at times, are too terrible for our consciousness to face in reality, so instead, we bury them or erase them, making them nothing at all. It seemed that I had inadvertently walked into one of those dangerous zones that my mind couldn't normally handle. But why did I think of it this way, and what exactly was this place?

Regaining control of my emotions, I went down the hallway. I didn't know why, but instinctively, my hand shot to my hip where I was holding my gun. I assumed that whatever happened to me here was bad enough that I automatically felt danger. The inside of the house was broken down beyond recognition of my memories. Any upholstery on the furniture had long since rotted away, and mold had crept in, uprooting all of the wallpaper and paint. However, large swaths of the house were simply wood paneling, as was typical with the construction of these types of homes. From what I could see, a few pieces of furniture remained, showing visible signs from years of water damage and the elements.

A desk was sitting in the central living room, almost like an altar. This desk was confusing to see, and for a few seconds, I considered whether or not my mind was playing tricks on me. Perhaps I had once again regressed into a dreamlike state, or maybe I was hallucinating what I saw. But, no, that was not the case. In this ruined footprint of a once lived-in home, in this ghost of my past, I saw a beautiful desk that was utterly untouched by time, and on it was what appeared to be an open book, also new. Well, not truly new, for its pages were yellow with age and its spine tarnished by the sun, but it was open, and there was fresh ink on its pages. Common sense told me that a book, especially one left open, would be torn apart by the ravages of time, especially considering the water damage to the rest of the home. So again, I felt a sense of trepidation.

I edged closer to it and looked at its open page. There was a compilation of names listed with dates that were followed by instructions and notes under some of the names. I picked up the book and flipped through its pages to be met with more and more of the same dates, names, and locations. Occasionally, symbols would break it up or what seemed to be some form of a mathematical formula that I couldn't decipher. The small, neat handwriting was placed so that perhaps thirty names would appear on each book page, complete with location and other extraneous information about that person. An unnerving sense of fear washed over me, and suddenly, as if struck by an urge, I flipped back through it.

It was obvious that the book entries were written chronologically and that these dates corresponded to events, though I didn't know what they were. Fearfully, as I flipped through its dusty pages, a dull reminiscence of the book fluttered through my mind; if not this book exactly, then one very similar had been here on my previous visit. I was standing with the very ghost of an object out of my past. Out of curiosity and a growing sense of dread, I flipped the pages back as far as I could. Sure enough, the record went back to the early '80s. I flipped back to the most current page and read going back. It didn't take long before I started recognizing names and places, finding that a shocking number were in Bayfield.

Sometimes, revelations are not sudden. They don't hit you like a bolt of lightning. Instead, they begin to creep up on you, leaving you with a gut-wrenching feeling in the pit of your stomach. In this case, I fearfully recognized that these names were some of the same ones from the missing person's reports Luke had shown me back at Harry's.

It didn't dawn on me immediately once the cold horror spread fully throughout my body, but I couldn't keep it from taking control. My instincts said to run, but instead, I stood there feeling my heart racing as adrenaline pumped through my veins. I was suddenly jolted by a strange sound and realized it was coming from me. It wasn't a scream as one may expect, but a low moan or gurgle. It was an unconscious expression of the frenzied panic, turning my mind into a chaotic pit. At times, it's impossible to keep one's body from doing things like this, acting out in ways unexpected or unimagined, as I had come to learn this in life.

I'm not sure how long I stood in that position. I wrestled with my mind and body, trying to return to a frame of mind that would allow me to take action instead of numbly standing there. I knew that what I was holding must be crucial evidence and that I needed to get it away from this place, but I also knew that if this was simply here, lying around, then the house must be dangerous. In addition, it was also possible that there was more critical and even more damning evidence around. Though it wasn't in any grand internal monologue, I was trying to decide between investigating further or fleeing. Would I run from this damned, horrid house with what I had, or would I stay, confronting the terror and seeing what else I could find? Eventually, after the involuntary sounds had ceased, I took several sucking, shuddering breaths. I resolved that I needed more.

As terrifying as this evidence was in context, without further physical evidence, it could be thought that it was simply a sick prank or the ramblings of someone who happened to know about missing person cases. Something I learned during college was to have very little faith in the justice system unless you could provide them with overwhelming amounts of evidence for your claim. If the source could not be authenticated, the information could be considered hearsay and not believed. One could say it didn't happen if it wasn't in writing; however, all these names of missing people could provide documentary evidence in a court of law, but was it enough? With this in mind, I knew that I would have to push through my fear and move cautiously through the seemingly derelict halls of the building in search of anything else that I could use to support my case and make a more substantial claim. If nothing else could be found, I could at least take this book back to my department, though I thought the bureaucrats there may have tried to raise a stink about evidence from what was technically another jurisdiction.

Moving throughout the house, I realized how large it was. In fact, it was closer to a mansion than an average suburban dwelling. As I moved through the halls, more vague memories of the occasion when I must have been there floated through my head. Considering the circumstances, I tried to pay them very little attention, at least as little as I possibly could, as I wanted to be alert as I searched. Soon, it became apparent to me that there was something else strange about the abandoned haunt. Though it initially appeared to be neglected and subject to the normal weathering you would expect from a house left to the elements, a more thorough examination showed that this impression was only superficial. Perhaps my thoughts were being colored by the discovery of that book, but to me, it seemed as though the house was somewhat elaborately staged.

As though its seeming state of disrepair was a careful forgery, and all essential functions were being preserved, I saw no exposed wiring nor any place where the flooring was badly damaged enough that I had to choose my steps carefully. There was no loud creaking from the floorboards, nor was the water damage extensive enough that any of the ceilings had collapsed. To sum all of my observations up, this was a house made to look old and dirty rather than a house that had genuinely been left to the mercy of the elements. This observation, of course, came with a secondary, immediately threatening implication. Namely, if it was simply being staged to look abandoned, then one could assume that the house was still in use. But for what?

The presence of the book had already proved that there were people who came here who used the space, at least from time to time, but it didn't say anything about what the space was being used for. Grimly, I considered the idea that this could be a hideout of sorts or perhaps a place where victims were taken before their final resting place; however, I would assume that a place like that would show more signs of struggle. I dismissed the thought, but I had such little information to go on. How many people were involved in this? Was it a lone stalker, or perhaps a pair? It was possible, of course, that all of this was tied to human trafficking. If so, this would be larger than anything I could handle. Still, though, I needed to do my part. Turning the corner to the left, I was met by a sight I had not expected.

As a part of the apparent weathering, most of the doors in the house were either off their hinges or on the floor, hanging loosely open or altogether gone. But here, on the underside of a staircase, almost certainly leading down to a lower level, was a large and particularly ornate wooden door. If I had to guess, I would have thought it was made of oak. It was not just the fact that the door was standing and closed that surprised me; rather, it was its condition. The door was aged, though it had been cared for, and the hinges were new. It was new enough that I couldn't see signs of rust, and its brass doorknob was almost smooth from current use. Most striking, however, was the addition of strange-looking symbols adorning the entirety of the surface of the door. Some of them were fresh and looked like they had just been painted.

Others were faded and old. It was impossible to tell how many coatings of these symbols were made or with what substance they were painted. Some appeared to be painted like a large sacred bird, surrounded by a ring of fire containing italic numbers painted of varying colors. Others were made of a duller substance, almost dark brown. I recognized with a shudder that this was roughly the correct color for dried blood, but it was evident that there was some symbolic or ritual meaning to the symbols adorning this hallway and door.

They were put together with extreme care and specificity, and the geometric qualities of the symbols were exacting even in those that appeared to be written out in bodily fluids. At this point, I think I had become somewhat detached from the situation. My consciousness moved back from the front to a more passive observing role as my body took its place on the front line of dealing with the brunt of the stress of the situation. This was also a good thing because I wasn't sure how I would have reacted if I had been fully aware of my surroundings when looking at that door. I froze as I heard faint footsteps from underneath me.

11

Those next moments were a complete and utter blur.

I couldn't run for fear that I would be heard, and so, with great care, I tried to quietly move to another piece of the house as far as I could get from the door. Moving quietly and quickly do not mix well, though, and by the time I heard a series of locks being undone and the turning of the handle, I was only two rooms away. Thinking quickly, I looked at the shabby furniture pieces, finding an overturned wardrobe amongst them. I crawled into it, closing the doors as much as I could, hoping that the small creaking noises would not alert whoever was coming up from that chamber to that room.

I just sat there motionless, trying to be as silent as humanly possible. Even my breath and heartbeat felt as though they were colliding forces. I thought for sure that they could hear me. They must be mocking me, walking through the halls, not approaching the room right away, but from my hiding space, I could hear them moving, but more importantly, I could hear them speaking.

"Is it really necessary to patrol the grounds? You know as well as I do that no one is interested in this place."

Another voice responded to the first. "You say that now, but you need to remember that people like rummaging through abandoned buildings. Junkies, explorers, sometimes just teens looking for a place to hang out and drink."

"Yeah, well, it's been a while since I've seen any sign of trespassing. I'm just saying that something feels strange."

"Yeah, sure, it's strange, but when a higher-up tells you to be on the lookout, you can't just ignore them, right?"

The idea that this place used to be frequented by people with no ties to what was happening and that there were poor people who would come here on accident sent shivers down my spine as I wondered what became of them. At the same time, however, my focus was on the other piece of their conversation—the insinuation that someone had contacted them and warned them to be on guard. It didn't sit right with me. It led me to a far-fetched conclusion, but one that I couldn't disprove. Perhaps it was self-centered or delusional, but I believed that the current circumstances called for some degree of paranoia, all things considered. It seemed to me that someone had warned these people about my presence. How they would know about it, I had no clue. After all, I had told no one about my prospective trip.

Only one possibility popped into my mind. Perhaps Luke, when he had given me the information, had let associates know about my interest in exploring this place. I cursed to myself in my head, thinking how stupid I had been to follow up on a stranger's lead, especially when that stranger had shown themselves to be so resourceful and threatening. That didn't matter now though. At that moment, I needed to focus on evading detection and escaping. I strained my hearing to try to figure out where the men's movements were coming from. Though I had only heard two voices, that wasn't proof that there were only two men, and indeed, through straining my hearing, I could detect at least three people. Their heavy footsteps meant they were wearing boots, I thought, but there was another sound that came with them. It was an unsettling sound, like they were dragging something behind them, and they were displacing objects as they were moving. I thought they were probably wearing robes or dresses, something that would trail behind them and move all the little pieces of wood, debris, and glass in their wake.

The question remained in my mind, freshly burning: who were these people, and what was their objective? I heard one of the men, the first one I had heard speaking, call out, seemingly in anger and panic. "The book's gone!" There was a real commotion and a flurry of footsteps. It sounded as if they had started to run.

"What do you mean it's gone? It can't just disappear." The man's voice was quivering with fear; he was obviously in a frenzy. Why was this book so important to them? Of course, it could be incriminating, but what I had read didn't include the names of the writers, at least, not that I could tell. It was just a hunch, but I got the feeling that there was something particularly special about the book. The symbols inside of it and on the door were helping me form a theory. It seemed probable that I was dealing with a group of fanatics of some sort, perhaps a cult. That was nothing though. I didn't know who they were, what they were doing, or why.

I was dealing with too many unknowns to have confidence in anything, and then it came to mind that I was thinking about this while huddled in an overturned wardrobe. It seemed utterly absurd that this was where I would be placing my mental energy. Looking back on the event later, I would come to realize that my odd behavior and thoughts were my mind trying to cope with the shock of the situation, and I had to stifle myself from crying out loud at the strangeness of it all. Thank goodness, though, I was successful in my attempt and kept quiet. In the other room, the men were becoming more frantic, and I could hear them tossing around the decrepit furniture, trying to find the book I had cradled in my arms. Cold fear was growing even more than I thought possible in my chest as I was expecting what they would do if and when they found me. I was listening to see where they would go next and what they would do. Either they would head toward me and I would need to get even quieter and pray that they wouldn't look inside the dresser, or they would move further away, and I would be blessed with an opportunity to make my escape.

Suddenly, the second voice shouted out, "There's a car parked up on the road!" My blood ran cold in my veins. I thought I had parked the car far enough away from the house to avoid detection. They knew I was here or thought I was already out there. It was a flip of the coin, so I sat there in the tension, waiting for what they would do. I guessed they were looking out the window at that point, trying to find the car the voice spoke of. I could not stop other thoughts from invading my head. What if they left and slashed my tires or sabotaged the engine? What if I was completely trapped here? I would have to make my escape on foot. Any possibility I could foresee was terrifying, and all that filled my mind's eye was capture or death.

I heard at least three sets of footsteps but only two voices talking to one another. Worrying still was that one of the voices was noticeably different from the others, and it had a shuffling gait, heavier than the rest. It seemed like it was the one dragging something, and some primitive part of my brain told me that this was the figure that was not speaking. My mind was racing and going wild, trying to fill in the blanks of what this figure was like. The others were men, though their voices were strangely muffled. Who was the third figure, and why were they so quiet? The unknown is always worse than really knowing, especially in such a high-stress situation, and as I sat there in the darkness, listening, my mind filled in the blanks for me in the worst possible ways. Again and again, like a movie repeating the same scene, the faceless officer with his pasted-on smile would stare down at me, and the strange thing walking up the trail toward me would appear. But now, I imagined that same ambiguous figure, shapeless and strange, only vaguely human and indescribable, was stalking the halls alongside the two men.

After moments of waiting, I could hear them all begin to move. They weren't coming closer; by a stroke of luck, they were moving further away, probably toward the front door. I wanted to breathe a sigh of relief but couldn't, fearing that any sound could bring them back. So instead, I focused on making hushed, quiet movements. I slowly pushed open the wardrobe door as it creaked ever so slightly. I winced and knew I had to move now.

Treading softly through the room and trying to avoid any large pieces of debris, I moved through the house; my pace quickened as I could feel my closeness to escape. Just as I thought I was in the clear, my heel came down on broken glass with a crunch. I heard movement at the end of the hallway. My stomach dropped as I recognized the footfalls as those of the third, silent figure. I whirled around to see a stark hooded figure that came straight from my nightmares. Standing there, wrapped in a red robe, dirty and stained, he had just rounded the corner. He wore a simple mask and a hood that looked like a black, tattered sheet pulled tightly around his face.

The man was tall and wide, almost to the point of being unnatural. By my estimate, he must have been nearly seven feet in height, and his shoulders took up nearly the width of the hallway. Worst were the beady eyes, visible through holes in the mask. I couldn't make out any pupils; instead, it was as though I was looking into the eyes of an animal. They reflected light in the dim hallway as though two searchlights were pointed in my direction; the moment of eye contact lasted a small eternity as I tried to get my body to run and waited for him to break into a sprint. That would never happen.

12

A thunderous sound escaped behind this sinister-looking thing as I heard a loud thud followed by the splintering of wood. The figure turned back toward the sound, and I ran to my left. As I passed through the doorway into the open central hall, I suddenly froze, witnessing the scene unfold. There were two other figures in robes, though they were more reasonable in their proportions and looked, for lack of a better term, normal. They started backing away from the front door, which had just been kicked off its hinges. In the doorway stood a figure silhouetted by the sun shining in through the opening. The figure shouted in a voice I recognized but could not immediately place, "Get your hands up and get down on the ground!"

I couldn't tear myself away from what I was seeing as my psyche implored me to run and take cover behind the far wall. As I did, the two men fell further back into the hallway, reaching into their robes and pulling out knives. Evidently, they weren't quick enough, as a deafening series of cracks suddenly split the air and made my ears ring. It was too loud to count accurately, and I was too busy covering my ears, but I knew the abrupt call of a .45 handgun when I heard it. The gunman had just fired into both men before they could get to him with their knives, a nearly impossible task at such short range. They collapsed into the filth of the dilapidated house like puppets with cut strings. Whoever this gunman was, he was truly skilled.

The air was hazy and pungent now. Mere moments after the shots were fired, the air was filled with the smokey charcoal and ammonia scent of burnt gunpowder. My ears were splitting, and I knew the next few hours would sound dull and filtered. I'd qualified with my handguns on the range for the police force. I had taken a few trips to the range on off hours just to maintain the same level of proficiency as when I received my certification. Still, I had never been involved in a defensive shooting, nor had I ever heard the sound of a gunshot so close without hearing protection. At the time, it seemed that the only thing keeping me going and functioning as well as I had been was pure adrenaline.

The sound and smell reminded me of something that had left my mind when I heard the men emerge from the basement. My hand shot to my holster, pulling my own handgun free. In the commotion, I had forgotten that I was armed. Perhaps it was the feeling of being transported to the past that had washed over me when I entered this place, but any thoughts of self-defense or the singular obsession to find the truth were overridden when I entered that ghastly place.

As my hearing began to return, the first thing I could make out was more sounds coming from underneath me. With a sickening dread, I realized there must be more people downstairs who hadn't traveled up initially. The silhouette seemed to realize this and broke into a sprint toward the symbol-marked door, overturning a desk and barricading the opening. The man looked up, and now I could see his face, though he hadn't spotted me yet. "Olivia! Where are you?" It was Luke.

I leveled my gun at him and called back, "I'm right here. Now put your gun down; you have a lot to explain!"

Luke sighed and stood up from the barricade he was making. He hadn't dropped his gun, but he also wasn't pointing it at me; at least that probably meant he wasn't here to try to kill me. "What are you doing here?" I asked.

He looked over at the two bodies with a dumbfounded expression on his face. "Well, I came to make sure you were alright and be a backup if you found yourself in a dangerous situation." Luke was surprisingly casual for a man who had just shot two people. It could have been shock, but instinct told me that wasn't the case. This wasn't his first shootout; that much was for sure. Aside from that, though, his story wasn't piecing together, and I needed the missing pieces to make sense of it all.

"How did you know I'd be here today? Aside from that, how did you know that I was in trouble? Have you been following me?" I liked to think that I was very aware of my surroundings in day-to-day life. After all, I was an investigator. It wouldn't be easy to get under my radar, which meant that either he had found some way to track me from afar or he was extremely good at trailing people. I wondered who this man really was who had suddenly appeared in my life.

"Maybe I followed you here, but that was for the best, right?" Luke was smiling now. As strange as it may seem, something about how he handled the situation put me at ease. By all means, I should have been petrified by this maniac who very well may have been stalking me, but there was a warm nostalgia exuding from his actions. I couldn't place it, but there was an unshakable feeling that I could trust him despite everything my senses and rational thoughts told me. There was muffled banging at the marked door, and I knew that if we were going to leave, there was no time to waste.

I turned back toward Luke to warn him we had to leave. As I turned my face toward him, my eyes grew wide; his gun was up and pointed at me. His expression was one of fear and malice, and it didn't make any sense. My blood froze in my veins. How could I have let my guard down so quickly when I had just been holding him at gunpoint? I already knew I was dead, and I had no time to react. All I could manage to do was close my eyes and brace myself as his fingers squeezed the trigger.

The stench of fear hung in the night air, and my ears rang, but I felt no pain. I opened my eyes again to see Luke continuously firing. He was shooting directly over my right shoulder. I whirled around to see his target, only to be met with the same gargantuan creature of a man lurching in the hallway before. Without much thought, my body recognized that this was a threat that couldn't be dealt with by one man alone, and I instinctively leveled my pistol, firing into the colossal man's center mass.

When we are first taught to handle firearms, investigators and police are told about how lethal their service pistols can be. The chance of killing someone with a single shot to the chest using a handgun chambered in .45 ACP is near 90 percent. There are, of course, statistical exceptions to this rule. Sometimes, you'll hear about people surviving far worse wounds, but in general, a human cannot withstand the raw traumatic damage of bullets in any capacity. With this in mind, one can imagine my fear as the monstrous robed figure continued to stroll, almost casually, toward us after we had shot him approximately seven times in the chest. He hadn't made a sound, nor had his movements changed.

The only proof we had hit our mark was the trickling blood oozing from the bullet holes in his robes. I was too absorbed in the moment and in my ever-growing state of shock to notice that I had run out of bullets. I continued to pull a locked trigger on an empty magazine and was only saved from the steadily advancing monstrosity by Luke grabbing my shoulder and screaming into my ear . . . "RUN!"

I want to say that I protested. I want to say that my principles for discovering what was happening overrode my sense of personal safety. As much as I would love to say that, that's not what happened when I was given that command. I ran, and I ran quickly, directly in tow with the sharply dressed gunman. We sprinted down the dirt driveway, into the road, down the block, and past my car until we found a black sedan. Luke called for me to get in, and as I was thinking at the time, I didn't protest. Some faraway corner of my mind made a mental note that it was a very nice car, certainly far too nice for an independent detective to be driving around in. We were moving in no time, and I was left sitting there as the house disappeared into the horizon behind us. Just before we drove out of view, I could see a tall, statuesque, and horrific figure casting a dark shadow in the doorway on the front porch, and I just thought, though I could not be sure, that there were far more warped silhouettes in those old shattered windows.

It took perhaps thirty minutes of driving until we were well out of that old rural neighborhood and back into the familiar Gainesville streets for my heart to start slowing down and my mind to begin processing information normally. I took account of my situation from the top. I was sitting here with a journal marked with names, notes, and symbols I had taken from that house. I was in an oddly nice car with a man whom I had just witnessed shoot three people, and I was suddenly hit with the shocking realization that I had also shot someone. In going over these facts, I was attempting to rationalize them or make sense of a narrative where there was none. To this point, the drive had been in complete silence, though I was becoming aware of the fact that I was occasionally whimpering and sniffling. I had been crying without realizing it.

Perhaps Luke had been paying attention to my crying and noticed that I had slowed down, or maybe he had observed my body language. Or was it possible that simply out of coincidence, that was the moment Luke decided to speak to me? "Okay, Olivia, I know you're probably pretty shaken up about what happened back there, but I think it's obvious that we need to have a conversation." His voice softened and hinted that while he had adrenaline pumping through his system, he was nowhere near as upset as I was. It took me a few minutes to gather my thoughts and express my feelings.

"Yeah, we do. I have some questions for you."

The sharp-looking man glanced around the lots and strip malls we were going past until we arrived at an intersection. He turned to me with a half smile. "Sure, I think now's the time for me to give you some answers, but I'm starving, and that diner looks pretty good. How about you?" He motioned to a '50s-style diner, the sort that was all chrome and vintage furniture. I hadn't thought about it until then, but the ordeal in the house left me quite hungry, though common sense told me this wasn't the proper thing to do after such a traumatic event. I was still enveloped in the unreality of adrenaline and shock, and pancakes sounded nice.

I didn't really have a smart way of answering his question without laying my cards on the table. "You know what? Sure, I'm hungry. Let's eat."

"Nice!" He had a big, goofy grin on his face, and now, in the afternoon light, I got a good look at him for the first time. By every measure, Luke was a very handsome man, to the degree that I was surprised it wasn't more apparent before. Perhaps I had been too worried about what he had been saying last time to really notice him. His eyes were a vivid green and he had chiseled features and the kind of light five o'clock shadow that showed a man who usually took very good care of his personal hygiene but was still a little rough around the edges. His dirty blonde hair was side-swept with a shaved undercut, the sort of hairstyle you usually see in professionals who don't have time to fuss with their looks but still take pride in their appearance. Besides all that, though, I just couldn't shake the warm nostalgia surrounding him. Usually, when things remind me of the past, it was terrible. It always meant that I was reminded of sadness or horror, but instead, there was warmth and genuine comfort in this mysterious man's presence.

As we entered the diner, I fell into the booth and felt like my body was lead. I was drained and tired but curious and hungry enough to offset the growing exhaustion. It took no time at all for a waitress to come up and take our orders for drinks. After a few minutes, I sat beside Luke, sipping on a soda while he stirred his coffee. It seemed like as good a time as any to start asking my questions. "Who are you really, and what do you do? You're certainly not a private investigator."

13

Luke looked up at me again, a smile on his face.

"Well, you have me there. That's true. I'm not a PI. Maybe it would be best for me to reintroduce myself, this time without keeping anything from you." He playfully straightened his tie before extending his hand for a handshake. I would have found this behavior annoying from anyone else, but something about it was a bit charming or cute coming from the man I had just recently seen as a serious force to be reckoned with. When I offered my hand, he took it and firmly shook it, introducing himself as if it were our first time meeting. "My name is Luke Hayes, and I'm an agent with the FBI." He reached into his breast pocket with his free hand, producing a badge. My jaw went slack. What, he was an FBI agent? Of all of my guesses and theories, that wasn't one of them.

"Wait, wait, so you're also law enforcement? Why didn't you just contact me through the police station then?" It would have certainly been easier for him to have just gotten in contact with me through the department. Going through the trouble of leaving out personal details and meeting me without disclosing he was an FBI agent didn't make sense unless . . . perhaps there was a reason to avoid the local police.

"Tell me, Olivia, before I came along, have you had any luck whatsoever trying to get leads in the Paige Phillips case?" Just like that, his smile was gone, and suddenly he was all business. The answer was obvious, though: I hadn't had any luck with it. That's why I had taken the chance to meet someone I didn't know, like him. He continued, "I won't get too deep into why, but let's just say I didn't want to deal with your particular police department. I've found them extremely difficult when dealing with missing person cases, and that chief of yours has a very forward-thinking attitude and tends to leave those forgotten to remain forgotten.

I guess what I'm trying to say is that it was easier to get in contact with someone passionate and assertive than to use authority to go over the heads of people who I knew would make my life difficult." I supposed that made some sense. I hadn't heard of anyone being able to get a cold case opened at the police department. No doubt Luke, or rather, agent Luke Hayes, could have used his authority to get whatever information he wanted, but he definitely would have received pushback. That still didn't answer all of my questions though.

"From what you showed me, it seems like you have plenty of information already. I don't think you needed me to find more. My question to you then becomes, why did you seek me out?" Luke sipped his coffee and stared deeply into my eyes. I was usually very good at reading people, figuring out what was happening inside their heads, but not him. It was different. I couldn't tell at all. Normally, that would be scary, but there was something nice about it in this case. It was like I was genuinely talking to someone on my own level, without all the mind games, as strange as that was to think, given the circumstances.

After a few moments, it became obvious that he struggled to find words to explain himself. This was surprising to me. For whatever reason, I had assumed he was collected enough to always have a ready excuse or an explanation. The revelation that he was trying to figure out how to communicate with me conscientiously was not insignificant. I suddenly became very aware that the person I was talking to was not just the physical embodiment of a law enforcement agency, nor a shady character, but a person. As he struggled to find the words, the waitress came with our food. This seemed to loosen him up as he took another sip of coffee. "I don't have any way I can twist this, so I'm going to be straightforward with you. I believe that you are the person who is key to unraveling this case. Not just for Paige Phillips but for a lot of other people. You're the only person here who I can trust." There was a hint of sadness in his voice at the end of his statement. I got the feeling that trust was perhaps something Agent Hayes didn't come across much in his regular line of work.

As I cut into my pancakes, I couldn't help but chuckle. "Really, I'm the only person you can trust? Luke, you don't even know me." I looked up from my plate to see an expression of deep sorrow plastered on his face. I wasn't sure exactly what I had said to elicit it, but something resonated deeply with him and made him sad. It was true though; this man had come from nowhere and simply offered me information. Up until today, I had thought of him as strange and mysterious at best and dangerous at worst. The only reason I felt comfortable enough to sit down at this meal with him was he had seemingly saved my life.

Luke seemed to be biting his tongue. It was as if he wanted to say something but simply couldn't. "I understand what you mean, but from my point of view, you were the right person for this job; however, I truly regret that I put you in harm's way. I'm sorry."

"So you're saying you didn't mean for me to go to a place filled with robed, knife men and giant monstrosities?" I was angry saying it, but I also realized how absurd the statement was, just on its own. In the intervening seconds of silence, he looked back down on his plate and stifled a laugh.

"I suppose that's one way to put it, Olivia. I didn't want you to get into harm's way at all. According to all of my intel, that was a location that should have been abandoned. I thought you could just go there and it might jog some memories." I put down my fork. What he had just said was huge. Why would that place have jogged my memories? It did, of course; I had been there before, but how would he know that, and consequentially, why would he know that? Why would he be sending me to places that would help restore that lost childhood time? I knew he wouldn't be completely honest with me, so I would need to extract answers little by little. There was one thing that I bet I could get him to say though.

"What was that place?"

Luke took a moment to think while chewing his scrambled eggs, placing his fork and knife down, and pushing the plate away from him. He reached down to his side, picked up his briefcase, and laid it on the table beside the plates. "Officially, that house is abandoned; however, there are no routine checks done there to check for people like squatters. It also seems to be entirely ignored by local law enforcement. As far as I can tell, it is an operating house for a rather large cult that is active in the tri-state area. This cult is at the very center of my investigation. While the house is now abandoned, or was supposed to be, that was not always the case. Twenty-two years ago, it was owned by a Mr. Cooper Harrison."

When Luke said that the house was owned twenty-two years ago, he looked up at me, maintaining eye contact the rest of the way through. I did not know how to process what he was telling me, and in that state, I said the first thing that came to mind. "You're lying to me! I know Cooper Harrison, and I know that he was never in Gainesville." What I was feeling was a complex mixture of emotions, but most of them felt close to anger and confusion. This man had come into my life, sent me to someplace where I could have wound up dead, and was now trying to turn me against one of my closest family friends. I was beyond the point of losing it.

The FBI agent shrugged, unclasping the case and leafing through documents. "I can't blame you for being angry, but your anger is misplaced." He put a photocopy of a deed in front of me. "According to public records, that residence was owned by a Cooper Harrison." That's indeed what it said on the photocopied paper in front of me, but I thought it could possibly be a forgery. This could have been some way to try to gain control over me or put a wedge between me and one of my closest friends. My mind was reeling in shock.

Emotional exhaustion was beginning to catch up with me, and along with it came a torrent of anger directed at this man for putting me in such a situation to begin with. I pushed the paper back toward him. "You're full of shit!" There was no room for discussion in my voice. It was an absolute statement. Completely disregarding any of the warmth I had felt for him up to this moment, my feelings had now turned to nothing but disgust. Looking back across the table, I expected an aloof smile or a shrug, but instead, I saw the FBI agent's face was dead serious, displaying a tight frown, looking genuinely hurt and angry by what I had said.

"I'm trying to help you, Olivia, but I can't do that if you're going to be willfully ignorant. I sent you to that house for a reason, and I think you found it. You have the journal, don't you?" I had brought the journal in with me, placing it next to me on the booth bench. "I'm going to need you to pick it up and start flipping the pages back to twenty-two years ago." I tried to swallow but found that I couldn't. My throat was dry with fear. It was a simple request, and one that I could certainly oblige, but something inside me told me that I shouldn't, that I couldn't undo what would happen if I followed his directions.

As my hand was hovering over the book, I realized in a moment of clarity how absurd the situation was. I drew my hand away from the journal, placed it back on the table, and glanced at Luke. Now, my gaze was piercing. "You know what, Luke? I'm not reading this. Not right now, at least. I won't dance on a string like a puppet and just do what you tell me. That's not who I am." Luke's eyebrows raised. He looked surprised, like he had never even considered that I would refuse his directions.

Seeing that I had gained some leverage in the conversation, I pressed on, "Before you, my investigation might have been going slowly, but now I feel like nothing but a pawn in some big game you're playing. Well, guess what? I'm not going to play along. I understand you might be investigating a cult, but that's none of my business. My business is finding Paige Phillips. And let me tell you another thing. I don't know what kind of resources you have at the Bureau, but I know Cooper Harrison as well as my own father, and he would never do anything to hurt me, and he certainly wouldn't have had anything to do with what I saw today!"

There was an entirely new expression on Luke's face, a dark, unhidden anger. Perhaps he was angry that he had failed to manipulate me. "Olivia, are you telling me you have no memories of that house?" A chill went down my spine.

"Well . . . yes, I remember being there, but if it really was Cooper's house all those years ago, then, well, I don't know. I don't have the best memory. Maybe I mixed up the dates when we met him. Maybe Dad and he were friends before the move."

The look on the agent's face was a mixture of pity and frustration. "You didn't know Cooper Harrison before you moved to Florida, Olivia. Just think about what you're saying. Do you think that a man of his means owned a second home? Do you think that he moved to Florida with you? Neither is the case." I felt like he was making fun of me, like he was toying with me, and all that did was make me angrier.

"I'm not going to sit here and be manipulated, okay? I don't know what mind game you're playing, but I will continue to look for Paige in my own way."

Luke looked down at his food, clasping his hands together. He shrugged and then nodded his head. "Well, Olivia, that's entirely your choice; however, I have to give you a piece of advice if that's the direction you're going to go in."

I was already starting to get up from the table. "I don't think I need any more advice from you." To my shock, his hand shot forward, grabbing me by the shoulder. His face was one of sincere concern, though ominous.

"Sorry, but you really do. Take this." He thrust another file into my hands. "You have come to a crossroads now, and I'm explaining what the circumstances are. You have two directions that you can go in. Either you return to your life as it was, forgetting about what happened today, forgetting about Paige Phillips, and trying to go on with life. Or, if you're too proud to do that and have too much of a sense of righteousness and justice to let what's going on continue, you can open that file. I will tell you right now that unless you open that and read what's inside, your chances of ever finding Paige are virtually nonexistent."

14

I couldn't sleep that night. It had been four days since I had gone to that horrible house. And since I had talked again with Luke, I hadn't seen anyone in the department about what had happened. After we had talked, Luke still needed to drive me back, promising that he would have other agents retrieve my car, which they did. He had told me to keep quiet about it. If not for his sake, then for my own, as this was part of a larger federal investigation that didn't concern my jurisdiction.

As for the men and the shootings, he assured me that such things would be categorized and swept under the rug, so to speak, although he didn't go into details at length. Apparently, the way the FBI saw it, if a few people end up dead in investigating a dangerous group, that's expected and acceptable collateral damage. The entire event still felt like a fever dream, or quite distinctly a nightmare, but looking across my room at the oversized recliner, I could see the file and the journal, completely real and close.

On that night, I had come to a conclusion. I loved Paige Phillips just as much as I would have loved my own sister; however, I didn't know what was happening in this major investigation. It was too large and too dangerous. I would continue my quest on my own terms and look for leads the old-fashioned way. I didn't need to get involved with whoever Luke Hayes was, and I certainly didn't want to be caught in any more situations like the shootout at the abandoned house.

This resolution, of course, did nothing to bring me peace in the days following. I remember the day after I had gone back. I had taken Sunday off to rest, but all I could think about was the fear of confronting Coop on Monday. Another sleepless night left me drained and irritable, but I didn't care. I wanted answers. When I knocked on his door and let myself in, the air and atmosphere inside his office were far different than my usual experiences. Gone was the warmth and friendliness; instead, an overwhelming air of fear and trepidation dominated the space. I knew his initial reaction was strange, but if I was going to play devil's advocate inside my head, I supposed I would also be somewhat stunned if someone had dug up my old home from over twenty years ago. Coop stared at me from behind his desk; his expression was utterly blank, and he seemed resigned in some way, and all he had to say to me was . . . "So, Olivia, did you find anything useful?"

I could have been honest about what had happened. Still, considering my conversation with Luke and how much I wanted to put all of the events behind me, I decided that it would be best to avoid the situation altogether. I shrugged. "No, nothing really, just an old house."

"You know, Olivia, there's a whole lot of things that are okay for you to look into, and there's a whole lot of things that I think are fine for us to talk about, but there's a certain point where you cross a line into things that are . . . uncomfortable." Maybe he had a point. How would I have felt if a friend was digging into my past? Perhaps he was so uncomfortable that past week because he was fearful that I would dredge up certain personal things in his past that he didn't want to confront in the present. It was none of my business. I had always trusted him. It was a convenient and comforting answer, and so it's what I decided I would believe.

"Sorry about that, Coop. Trust me, it won't happen again. I just had some things confused." For the first time in a week, Cooper Harrison smiled at me.

"That's good. You were getting me all worried there for a bit!" He laughed, and the warmth that normally came from him returned to the room. I was still uncomfortable, but it was better. Some part of me felt like I had woken up from a strange, long dream that I had been stuck in for the past several weeks. It's that sensation of relief that you get when you enter back into reality, realizing that there is no monster lurking after you if things make sense. There were already so many stressful things I had to deal with in my life without worrying about larger conspiracies or menacing robed figures, but I found little comfort in this. At the same time, all I could see in my mind's eye was Paige frowning and shaking her head. I swore that I wasn't abandoning her, that I still was looking, that I was still hot on her trail. Those thoughts did little to comfort me.

The next few days and weeks were relatively calm. I decided to invest some time into spending more of my days off with Rebecca. She had an uncanny knack for finding the best spots in town for food or drinks, so going out with her became a regular habit. Sometimes, we would bike or hike to our destination. The two of us had become quite close, although at times, I wondered why she stuck so close to me. By all accounts, she was a far more exceptional detective and had been at the station for longer than I had. There was nothing officially tying us together as partners either. She seemed, at least on the surface, to simply like my company. I was glad; I really needed a friend at that time.

Eventually, my life got back to the point where I could almost forget what had happened during my typical waking day, ignoring things and keeping busy with my workload and my growing list of hobbies. I had taken up knitting and was starting to learn to bake. Rebecca was helping me realize that she was a wizard with an oven. With a nice friend and, of course, solid support from Coop and even the occasional call from Dad, I was, on paper at least, doing well.

Although not entirely out of mind and out of sight, I could see the journal and folder sitting on my recliner when I returned to my apartment every night, as if they watched or taunted me. I wanted nothing to do with their contents. Every time I looked at them, I was reminded of the mysterious agent who, no doubt even now, was tailing me. I couldn't get Luke out of my mind, as well as everything else. The names of the missing people haunted me, and the men in robes, especially that tall, silent man. The more I thought about him, the less I wanted to.

I couldn't shake the feeling that I had witnessed something far beyond what I should have. Every night was filled with nothing but nightmares. Not that nightmares were new, as it was normal for me to drift back into the traumatic past that lived inside me, but this was different. It would be easy to count the times I had not woken up in a cold sweat in the past three weeks. In those dreams, Luke was always there, but of course, the robed men were also there in the background. Usually, it was the recurring event, twisted by my mind being there in that long, dilapidated corridor with Luke beating down the door and coming to my rescue.

There was always a warm nostalgia, but in my dreams, there was another figure hovering over him and over me, prancing through the air. I couldn't make out who or what it was until the thing in the robe appeared at the end of the hallway, and the other powerful being suddenly materialized in front of me and Luke, forming a barrier. That's the moment I realized it was Zeus. His presence was undeniable and as real to me as when I would encounter him as a child. That's always when I would wake up.

I thought to myself that the stress really must have been getting to me in ways that I didn't understand if I was so rattled that my childhood imaginary friend was coming back to serve his purpose as my protector, but then again, that was something to be thankful for.

It had been over a month since that incident when I went out on a call that would once again change my life.

15

Autumn was truly in full swing in Florida, not that it meant much in the Sunshine State.

Ever since the murder case, and certainly since our growing friendship, Detective Roan and I had taken to going on patrol together and investigating some of the same cases. We worked well as a team, which Chief Hudson applauded and encouraged, so it made sense. This morning, we were supposed to go and inspect a crime scene, but something about it seemed off.

Apparently, a couple of teenagers had wandered across a dead body inside an abandoned warehouse near the station. Of course, evidence would need to be collected with any factual information and a motive from potential witnesses in the area to create a profile of possible suspects. However, this step of the investigation called for forensics, not us. I wasn't entirely sure why we were the ones being dispatched to take a look at the scene. As I usually did in these situations, I deferred to my higher-ups and simply went along.

The morning was chill, and it had only been several hours since the body had initially been found. I thought it strange that there wasn't anyone to respond sooner than when our shifts began. I was thankful for the cold air because there was no putrid smell along with the body, which was in a fresh state of decomposition that started immediately after death. The scene was terrible. A man in his young twenties, I would assume. The killing seemed to be ceremonial. It made my skin crawl, and not just in the usual way a crime scene did. There was something about it that didn't feel right. I couldn't place my finger on it precisely until, looking around, I saw a familiar symbol I had seen painted on the walls at the abandoned house like graffiti, using the victim's blood.

This brought back to mind the door with all the symbols where all of those robed men came from, and for a moment, I had to tell myself that I was overreacting, that I needed to calm down, but as I looked further, I realized that perhaps I wasn't being so rash after all. In fact, looking closer, I recognized several of those symbols.

"Geez, what a mess, huh?" Rebecca was talking to me, but I was staring off. I had a terrible feeling that I had gotten trapped in that spider's web I had been trying so hard to avoid. "Olivia, what's wrong? What's gotten into you? You're staring at that thing like it's a Picasso painting." One of the things I really disliked about Detective Roan, no matter how much I appreciated her and other aspects of her personality, was her casualness in these scenes of carnage.

"Can I be honest with you about something? Something dark." The detective was looking at me with those piercing eyes that she always had, but her face was an expression of approval.

"Of course. What's going on?"

I was trying to organize my thoughts, to figure out how I could express what I was seeing in a way that wouldn't make me sound insane or reveal what I was up to. Eventually, I decided that I couldn't avoid it, so I had to be honest. I sighed and returned to the squad car, retrieving from my bag the journal I had decided to bring for safekeeping. Opening it up, I found another copy of the same symbol written in blood. "Rebecca, I've been doing some investigating on my off hours, and I ran into some people at an abandoned house that seemed violent, some kind of cult, I think. They had this book with them, and those symbols that are written on the wall in this warehouse also show up in this book." I looked over toward my friend, expecting a look of disbelief or perhaps worry, but instead, I saw a blank stare.

"Okay, and what about it? I've seen plenty of killings where people leave symbols at the crime scene. Sometimes they're just religious, but most of the time, it's referencing something in a book or a movie, and you know criminals aren't the smartest sorts." I was completely taken aback. There was no way someone as smart as Rebecca would think this was just a coincidence; after all, this was a murder scene.

You couldn't just go and dismiss pieces of critical evidence so impulsively.

"No, Rebecca, listen to me. I'm telling you that these people are linked to multiple murders and disappearances. I don't know what these symbols stand for, but I know they're the calling card of a group of dangerous people. That means this is linked to something bigger than this crime." Rebecca's blank stare formed into a scowl. She looked annoyed or even more than annoyed; she was enraged.

"We don't have time to go over every little detail of the scene. What you're doing right now is wildly speculating. It doesn't matter if you have a book with a similar symbol in it. That is not a piece of evidence that we can use in a murder."

I felt like I was talking to a brick wall. How could she be acting like this? It was unbelievable. I needed to get my point across, so I tried in the only way I could to outline the importance of my findings. "Rebecca, please listen to me. This isn't just a book. It's a list. I've checked all the names in here. They're missing people! It shows where they came from and how they were taken, and some of them even have marks near them that indicate whether or not they've been killed. This is huge, and I'm telling you, this is part of it. You have to believe me!"

The change I saw creep over Rebecca's face was cunning and slow but so drastic and marked that I could not help but stand in awe. It was as though every vestige of the human emotions I usually associated with my friend were fading away, leaving only that uncomfortable, predatory gaze in a blank, robotic expression. "Olivia, I don't want to repeat myself. If I say it isn't important, it truly isn't important." Her voice was no longer tinged with anger, and her expression remained void of any worry or concern. It was a blank monotone with the thinnest edge that told me of a hidden danger, that these words had poison in them. Again, the pangs of worry were washing over me. I had spent the past month trying to bury the memories of what had happened, but I felt deep down that something was terribly wrong.

"Rebecca, I don't know what's going on, and I don't know why you're acting like this, but I need you to listen to me!" At this point, I was begging. I didn't even know if I was begging her or making a plea to myself and my trust in her, but whatever the case, I knew that I was demeaning myself. It didn't matter at this point though. I needed to be heard. I needed to know that I was not being betrayed. It was of such vital importance to me that this person I thought was my friend believed that I was speaking the truth. What reason would I have given her to make her think otherwise? I just didn't know if I could handle the surmounting sense of unreality coming at me.

Rebecca maintained eye contact while turning to her side and walked back toward the body lying by the wall with the painted symbols. It had always felt as though she was staring through me, or perhaps as if she was staring at prey, but now I truly sensed that I was in danger looking at her. No longer was it the sharp eyes of a hawk, but rather the hungry eyes of one of the most brutal predators, like a lion or tiger.

"Olivia, listen very closely to me. I am listening to you. I hear what you're saying. I am paying attention and telling you as a friend to stop crying. I am telling you that this does not matter and does not concern you. If you value our friendship, then you should listen to me right now and not interfere with what I'm doing. It would help if you trusted me as your closest friend and have trust that what I am doing is for your benefit."

I had never heard this tone of voice from Detective Roan. At times, she could be monotone; at others, she sounded like your average woman in her thirties, but now there was a velvety smooth texture to her voice, something soothing in its pitch and almost hypnotic or transfixing. My mind instinctively replayed all that had happened this past month and everything we had done together. My restless thoughts turned to my whole relationship with the detective, back to when I first met her. It suddenly occurred to me that I hadn't known Rebecca for very long—all things considered, only a few months—but I liked to think that we were quite close.

Somehow, I had overlooked her inherent strangeness. I struggled with my thoughts, trying to recall all of our outings and what we did outside of work, confiding in one another and offering support when needed. Those things had been, to this point, comforting me from the growing sense of strangeness that prevailed in every area of my life. Now, they took on a hue of grayness that felt forced and manufactured. I realized that I had been looking for comfort in places where there may have been none. Still, though, for a moment, even if a short one, I considered listening to Rebecca's advice. Perhaps I would be genuinely happier if I let all of this go and could just accept what was happening and stop worrying. It was a temptation, I'll admit, but not one that required any long consideration on my part.

I worked to steady my heart and produce a calm voice. "Look, Rebecca, I don't know what's going on here, but I trust you as my friend, so I need to tell you this exactly as the facts stand. I found this list. This book is from an abandoned house in Gainesville. There were definite signs of cult activity there, and that's where I first saw these symbols. I know you're not acting right. I know that you must know something about this, but I'm begging you, for the sake of our friendship and your own humanity, to at least tell me what's going on!" Looking back on it, this was perhaps the most foolish thing I could have done in my position. I should have known the danger I was putting myself in by telling her this, but I was blinded by a childlike optimism that came from this flourishing friendship. Or, perhaps it wasn't even that but a desperate hope for normalcy, some prevailing sense that life could return to how it had been. Maybe I was still holding on to that.

Rebecca sighed deeply, turning to face me, her hands on her hips. Her face was still in that mechanical, drawn look, but there was some level of humanity in her voice. She was using the kind of voice one would choose to scold a young child. It was matter-of-fact and condescending. "Has Coop ever told you that you can't let things go because you're terrible at it?

I only expected to do our walk-through, process the crime scene, and leave. Even with everything you have said up until now, I could have turned the other way or covered for you; after all, I considered you my friend. Instead, you just had to keep pushing until you left me no choice but to do this. Please remember, Olivia, that you brought this on yourself."

Before I could respond, or object, or do anything, with a skilled speed that spoke of her status as a veteran investigator, detective Rebecca Roan reached into her holster and drew out her gun, leveling it directly at me, safety off, finger on the trigger, legs bent at the knee; it was a tactical stance. I had seen her in this shooting stance several times when we went to the range together, and this was how she always pointed at a target before firing her entire magazine. At that moment, I knew that I was about to die.

16

What happened next was a blur and so quick that I was oblivious to the actual order of events.

There was intense noise, and I frantically recognized it as gunshots. I could smell the pungent sulfur lingering in the air but felt no pain. Then I realized the sound was coming from behind me, not in front of me. I don't remember seeing what happened at that moment, but I distinctly remember looking down to see Rebecca on the ground, her eyes still open, but she was dead. It took me a moment to compose myself enough to realize what happened. Before she could shoot me, someone had gunned down the detective.

I fell backward to the ground. The reaction was less based on instinct and more on the sudden revulsion of seeing my friend and comrade dead before my eyes. I had seen the men in hoods shot, which was the first time I had seen death happen and unfold right before my eyes, but even that had a layer of abstraction. I couldn't see their facial features or even their bodies. Here, I could see Rebecca crumpled before me like a paper doll. Her eyes were glazed over, and they stared off in different directions. The essence of death, brutal yet final, was so complete and perceptible. Even this person, whom I knew and cared for, looked exactly the same as the bodies of murder victims at the morgue. The thought threatened to overwhelm me, and I felt sick. Not long after, the horror of nearly being killed crept up on me. I whipped my head around, looking for whoever was responsible for the death of the detective I had considered my friend, a friend who had almost killed me. I didn't have to look far; behind me, a silhouette, familiar in shape, was approaching.

I didn't need to wait to see the familiar yet striking details of his face. The precise shooting, the telltale high pitch of the pistol, and the fact that it had happened so close to me in a time of danger already told me that agent Luke Hayes had been tailing me, in this case, just close enough. I turned to him, unaware of the tears streaming down my cheeks, only becoming conscious of it as I tried to speak through my shuddering and gasping, sobbing in ways that only someone racked with the guilt and fear of my situation could do. "You bastard!" I yelled out through the hoarseness of my swollen throat, wailing in fear, grief, and disgust. "Why? Why would you do this? Why would you take my friend from me?" I was hysterical. I realized it deep down, but I still felt it needed to be said. There were just so many emotions that I had been trying to process, trying to cram deep down inside, and I simply couldn't contain them anymore. The FBI agent was the only outlet I had, the only object I could turn my pain toward, and I was doing precisely that.

I felt like hitting him, throwing something at him, screaming at him as he grew closer. I was preparing every insult I could think of. I was going to thrust all of my heart at him to make him feel what I was feeling, but before I could do any of that, suddenly, he wasn't there, slowly advancing instead, diving forward, pulling me tightly into a hug. It was not the embrace of someone trying to win my affection or dodge blame; rather, it spoke of a sense of commitment and sorrow. It was an apology in physical form, and as I felt his body against mine, I could also feel his deep, shaking breaths and knew that he was crying. I didn't understand why he was crying, but I could hear him ever so softly next to my ear, repeating it like a spiritual chant. "I'm so sorry; I never wanted any of this for you." I didn't know what to do and felt nothing for a few moments, void of any perceptions and emotionally detached. Then, not knowing what else to do, I reciprocated the hug and pulled him in close, wailing and crying deeply. I think I stayed like that for a little while, though I couldn't say how long.

When he finally pulled away from me, our faces were red and puffy. My anger for him was still there, but in my heart, I also realized that he had just saved my life yet again. I repeated my question. "Why did this happen, Luke? Why did you shoot her?"

He looked at me as if he could see into my soul, not like the predatory, piercing look that I remembered Rebecca for, but with the sort of soulful gaze that spoke of unexpected reserves of empathy and understanding. That was exactly the issue though: I didn't understand who this man was or what I'd stumbled into. All I wanted to do was find out what had happened to my friend. Why was I now sitting next to the corpse of the woman I had thought of as my only female friend? Was this my fault? Was he to blame, or was it her? Or, perhaps all of this was simply fate turning against me, unstoppable in its tragedy. My father had never looked me directly in the face when I was angry with him. Boys I had always known never wanted to be the object of scorn or take any kind of responsibility. Even the men in the department would cover for their inadequacies, storming off, so there was, in a sense, a true impression made on me even in my grief-stricken anger and hysteria. Luke held my gaze, taking it all in as if he was fully accepting responsibility, even when, if truth be told, none belonged to him.

When Luke responded to me, his voice was low and gentle. There was no condescending edge to it, but there was an apology built into its tone. "It's because you would have died if I didn't do anything, and the only thing I could think of that would save you in time was to shoot. I'm sorry, it's my fault. I should have thought of something else, found another way, detained her, tackled her." He looked off into the distance and rubbed his eyes. "But I wasn't quick enough. I couldn't do what you needed me to." Of anything I had expected him to respond with, that was not it. Excuses, yes. Maybe a reprimand for my behavior. Perhaps a pep talk of some sort, but not this tearful, genuine apology. Something crossed my mind then. Why did it matter so much to him that I was determined to solve Paige's disappearance? Or was he interested in keeping me under close supervision as an eyewitness? How would he explain killing a seasoned police detective in cold blood otherwise? Was there something about me in particular that he was hoping to protect?

"I've asked this before, but I mean it. Who are you? Why is this happening to me?" Luke looked back toward me, and there was an indescribable sense of sadness and pain filling his expression and body language, like he wanted so badly to burst out and say something, yet he remained reserved. The agent stood up and walked the few steps over to where I had dropped the journal, reached down, picked it up, and brought it to me.

"I don't know how much of this you've looked into, but I'm assuming that it hasn't been much. As I said before, you had the option to either read it or try to return to normal life. I respected your decision to try to return, but now I think there's no going back. Please . . . look for the journal's section dated to the late '90s. I think you'll know what date to look for in particular." Perhaps it was due to the general mental exhaustion, but I had no more will left to argue or fight. At this point, I simply wanted to know what was happening, so I took the journal and began to look through it, searching for something I didn't know. It took a few minutes to find;

the journal wasn't always very clear in terms of dating. Some pages had many names, and others very few. Reading it closely, I recognized that all these people written down other than members were labeled as "candidates." Candidates for what though? I had no clue and wasn't even sure if I wanted to know. Still, I searched.

Despite what Luke had said, I didn't know what date to look for, but still, I found my eyes and fingers darting through the pages. Suddenly, my eyes became fixated on the wording before me: November, 1998. There was a name written down, and though some far-flung piece of me already knew what it would say, its confirmation made my heart sink to the pit of my stomach. It was written clear as day. For some reason, my brain refused to read the name, though I continued trying to. I looked at it repeatedly, but it simply didn't compute as I rolled over the syllables on my tongue. My head began to buzz and feel heavy. I looked up at Luke as he nodded. "Read it aloud," he said. I sounded out the syllables, and only when they were physically coming from my mouth did the horrible revelation fully hit me. It was then that my mind exploded into a firestorm of memory.

"Olivia Harper. November 1998." I am Olivia Monroe. I knew my name. I knew my dad's name. So why, when I said Olivia Harper, did I know it was me? Olivia Harper. I was Olivia Harper. I don't know when I stopped being her and when I became Olivia Monroe. Buried memories began to resurface, playing out in my head. I wanted to remember it all so badly, but would learning the truth be too much to bear? Feeling as if I would faint, my mind started to fold in on itself as I began to recall old steel tables and surgical lights. I remembered crying. I remembered men in hoods and robes that were so familiar and so very terrifying. I remembered my father, looking at him like he was a stranger.

I stared up at Luke, scared, wanting to ask questions but not knowing where to start, still trying to piece my mind together at its fringes. He had something in his hand, something he had pulled from his briefcase, and he was offering it to me. I silently shook my head back and forth, thinking I couldn't handle any more revelations, but he insisted, pushing it forward and nodding in the affirmative. I took the piece of paper and looked at it, a strained, sorrowful murmur of pure dread issuing forth from my raw throat. It was a missing person flyer, but the child represented on it was not Paige Phillips, but me. The name on it was Olivia Harper. I recognized my own picture. It was my first-grade school portrait from before we moved from Gainesville and before Mom had passed away. I slowly shook my head from side to side. No, this couldn't be happening. This wasn't real. I was having a nightmare, and soon I would wake up. I'd wake up to go and investigate with Rebecca. My world was not crumbling. I was who I thought I was. None of this was real. The desperate notions rang hollow in my head.

My body shook uncontrollably as a strange outburst of laughter came from my mouth. I knew that at the time, I had lost my mind. Luke propped me up against his shoulder and carried me out to his car. He had made a call while I was trying to process the information, and now more federal agents were swarming onto the scene, probably to deal with Rebecca's body or to make sure no one knew where I was. It was a minor concern, but somewhere in my mind, I wondered if witness protection would be a good idea. Would I need to testify in court? I only spent a small amount of time on these thoughts; they felt far away and irrelevant. My body pulsed and buzzed, my heart hammered in my chest, chills ran down my spine, and I felt myself dying, though I wasn't.

My ego was falling apart at the seams. Humans aren't meant to withstand this kind of mental stress, and evidently, there was a large amount of trauma that I had never even known about that was, sadly, coming through the floodgates on top of any other immediate source of my stress. In this ocean of thought and panic, I was struggling to keep afloat, and yet, strangely, the anchor that was there was that of the strong hands of the man next to me clasped tightly, supporting me. It was like a buoy keeping me somewhere familiar amongst the horrible storm at sea.

When I sat in the car across from Luke, the silence once again took over until I finally managed to look in his direction. Weakly, I asked the same question, only now I was beginning to have some idea of the answer. "Who are you?"

17

We arrived at a hotel on the outskirts of Bayfield.

I had said I wanted somewhere private for us to talk, and he agreed, so we were in a very nice hotel room. He had told me to make myself comfortable, though I had no clue how to do that at the time. So I just collapsed into one of the recliners in the corner of the room as he mirrored me, sitting close and bobbing his leg. For the first time since I had met him, he looked nervous. The only sound in the room was the air conditioner. Even though it was October, Florida has a way of giving you unseasonably hot weather when you least expect it.

Though the day had started cool, it was turning into a scorcher. I was happy with the air conditioning. Simple thoughts like that were taking over my mind; after all, what's one supposed to think about after seeing the death of their friend who just tried to kill them? Either your brain can cave in on itself in panic, drowning you in a downpour of adrenaline, or it can take you to a calmer place where the here and now rule.

I didn't find the silence uncomfortable, but I got the impression that Luke did. He was fidgeting in a way that was uncharacteristic of the few times I had seen him, wringing his hands, bobbing his legs, looking at different parts of the room, and surveying. After a few minutes, his eyes locked with mine, unable to contain his eagerness anymore. "I know you probably don't want to talk about this, and I'm sorry for being impatient, but I just need to know. What do you remember?"

It was a good question. I remembered a lot, and I also remembered very little. Everything was completely disconnected. Conflicting moments flung over some vast amount of time, or perhaps a very short amount, I had no clue. The analytical part of my brain that would normally give context to these images was completely gone. "I'm not entirely sure. I can remember more of the hooded people who looked like what we saw in Gainesville. I remember being taken somewhere. I remember being uncomfortable. I remember my name being different. There are a lot of other things that feel like they're at the door, struggling to break out, but I fear I don't have the mental ability to deal with it. Or maybe it's that I'm missing the information they need to be set free." Luke frowned. Perhaps that wasn't what he wanted to hear.

After a moment, the agent reached into his lapel, taking out a small device I recognized as a wiretap. He then disconnected it and looked at me. "I'm not supposed to do this. There's supposed to be a protocol for how this works, but I think I can help. Would you mind if we talked about your past?" I almost laughed. Of all the things I wanted to do, having a federal agent play therapist with me was not on that list. I was just taking a breath to tell him I was alright, but Luke blurted out before I could fully articulate my thoughts. "What do you remember about that day at the lake? The one where you and Paige were playing pirates?"

I looked over at him, shocked. His face was pulled into a tight, straight line. It was as though he had been waiting to say that for the past month. I'd never told him about any of my time spent with Paige. I'd never told anyone about our specific ways of playing. "How do you know about that?" Luke shook his head back and forth and cradled his head in his hands, rubbing his temples.

"Please just think about it. What did you do on that day? Was there anything that stuck out to you? Maybe you found something interesting or . . . ?" I thought about that day. It was one of my favorite memories with Paige and, unfortunately, the last of our playdates together. We had gone down to the lake to play pirates. She was the captain, and I was the first mate. We were searching along the shoreline for treasure. Zeus was there. I had very distinct memories of us, imagining him walking along by our side. But something else did happen now that he mentioned it.

I couldn't quite remember it. It was on the tip of my tongue. We had gone up the bank and found a trail, and then, going up the trail, I felt like we met someone. Yes, we met a little boy around our age, maybe a little older than us, though not by much. One or two years. I couldn't remember his face. I remember that he looked up at us, already digging at the stump of a tree. I had asked who he was, and he had said . . . My eyes suddenly went wide as my heart skipped a beat. I jumped up, ran over to Luke, and flung my arms around him. "Luke! Oh my God, Luke!"

Suddenly, it was all so clear what had happened that day. I remembered the face of the boy. He had stunning green eyes. His features, even at that age, were fine. He had sandy blonde hair. The little boy was named Luke Hayes, and he became the third person in our friend group, always sticking with Paige and me. I remember telling him about Zeus and him getting so jealous because he couldn't see our imaginary friend, and we always told him that he didn't have a sense of imagination. Of course, then he would just get more worked up. From that point on, the three of us were practically inseparable. It turned out that he went to our school as well. How could I have lost something so precious? How could someone I cared for so much simply disappear from my mind? What happened to me twenty-two years ago? As I hugged my old friend, I cried. He embraced me back, and I could feel that he, too, was wracked with emotion. It wasn't sadness this time or grief, though there were certainly elements of it in both of our actions. It was relief and happiness and a reunion long, long overdue.

Before I could say anything else, I heard Luke's voice strained with emotion. "I've missed you so much, Olivia." I felt terrible. I wished I could say I missed him, too, but I didn't even have the luxury of missing him. It was as though he had been erased from me. A part of my identity and past had just disappeared, so I couldn't make up for it other than the emotion I now felt. I simply nodded my head. There was something else that I remembered as I buried my head in his chest and cried, blushing from the memory.

Back when I remembered him, back before whatever had happened, I admit I had quite a childhood crush on Luke. Though, of course, at the time, I never could have imagined the man he would turn out to be. What was he doing here? How had he found me? Why was he so dedicated to protecting me? I needed to know all of this. As I looked up at those alluring eyes, I knew this discussion would be intense.

I was wracking my brain, searching for the right words to express my deepest and most burning questions. So many were competing for control in my head that I had trouble adequately choosing one. After a few false starts and a lot of deliberation, I decided on one I thought he would have a good, clear answer to. "Who exactly are we up against?"

Luke sighed. "If you're asking for things like how many members there are, where they came from, and how long they've been around, I couldn't tell you. I do know that they call themselves the Disciples of the Rising Phoenix.

We've only been able to take in a few lower-level initiates for questioning. All I can detect about their goals is that they believe they are helping humanity as a whole; however, as to how they're doing that, I don't know.

What we do know is that they are violent, that they abduct people, and that there's certainly a religious element to their crimes. The only other thing I can tell you about them, and this is particularly pertinent information in your case, is that they seem to be quite good at manipulating people. There is some evidence suggesting that they're masters of brainwashing and that they have the proper techniques in place to alter people's memories."

It was a good answer, and it gave me a lot to think about, though I had absolutely no concept of how I would possibly respond to it. If Luke was to be believed, and at this point, I was quite ready to believe him, my issues with my memory were not due to childhood trauma, at least not in the way that I had thought, but rather were the product of some form of brainwashing. I was apparently, at one point, a missing person. It then stood to reason that detective Rebecca Roan was somehow involved in this cult, and there were other implications that I knew I could make but was deemed not to at the time because I knew how unpleasant they would be. "Why would they target Paige and me? What possible interest could a cult like this have in a couple of little girls?"

Luke shrugged his shoulders, a look of genuine exasperation and bewilderment on his face. "Frankly, I have no clue. I've been trying to figure out what their MO was since

I joined up with the feds, and I'm no closer than when I started. It seems like their targets are chosen almost at random. Sometimes they're male, and sometimes they're female. Sometimes they're children or teenagers, and sometimes they're adults. Sometimes they're perfectly healthy; other times they have mental illnesses. Sometimes they're even on death's door. I can find absolutely no rhyme or reason for how they choose their victims. Unfortunately, most of these so-called candidates resurface later as members of the cult themselves, although others simply disappear, and I know for a fact that they have killed people."

The thought made me shiver. I didn't find it hard to believe that they had killed a fair number of people, considering my experience in that haunt of a house, and even this morning with my former friend. I lingered over what else I needed to know. Sure, there was a lot that I wanted to know, but I hoped that we would have a lot of time, and I needed to get the most important things out of the way first. One question shot through my mind, and I knew I had to ask it for Paige's sake and everyone else who had gone through whatever this was. "How can I help? And why did you come to find me in particular? I'm sure there were others who went through this who didn't end up back in the cult."

For a moment, I couldn't quite decipher the body language or facial expression Luke was making, and then I realized that it was a mixture of shame, sadness, and disbelief. "Why did I come for you, Olivia? I came for you because I've been looking for you for the past twenty years! One of my best friends goes missing, and what? Am I just supposed to accept it? No, I needed to find you. As far as you helping me, I think you have many buried memories. You probably know more about how these people operate than you realize. If you work with me, then I think we can figure out what these people are doing, where they are, and maybe, if we're lucky, how to stop them."

18

All of my life since Paige's disappearance, I had been singularly focused on the goal of tracking down what had happened to my friend.

I was, in essence, completely obsessed. I'd never had time for things like friends or hobbies, but my pursuit of trying to become the sort of person who could help find Paige ultimately led me to become a criminal investigator. None of that had prepared me for the realities of spending an extended period of time with someone I was quickly realizing I was falling for. I discovered that when it came to dealing with someone I found truly attractive romantically, I was, for all intents and purposes, a complete amateur. Thankfully, Luke's earnest personality helped me, considering I think he was oblivious to my blunders and awkwardness.

After all, he was overwhelmingly positive. I genuinely believe that finding me and triggering my childhood memories of him must have been a culmination of effort very similar to my lifelong search for my childhood best friend. At times I smiled to myself, thinking that if this was the kind of joy I had waiting for me when I got to the end of this long and painful road, then it really would be worth it. Of course, I couldn't help but think Paige may not have been as lucky as me. Maybe she hadn't simply been brainwashed. There was still the strong possibility, as there always had been, that she was laid to rest in a grave somewhere.

We spent a few days at the hotel trying to gather my thoughts and jog my memory more. There were quite a few things that I could remember by merely reminiscing about the childhood memories of our past. Still, vital information was difficult to come by, partially because of my will to concentrate and knowing I would never see Rebecca again. On the fourth day of our hotel stay, Luke returned with lunch and an interesting idea. I was starting to learn his little eccentricities. I've always been good at determining how people were thinking, reading body language, and that kind of thing. It was part of what made me a good criminal investigator. When Luke was excited, he got a particular skip in his step. Aside from that, he always developed a slight grin, the sort of dreamy look you would expect from a child hatching a plan. There was something very charming about the expression, but it also made him very easy to read.

As Luke sat at the table and laid out our sandwiches, I leaned forward and said, "So what exactly do you have planned?" He looked up at me, surprised. I hadn't let on that I had been learning his nonverbal cues, and though I'm sure he knew that it was one of my skills, he wasn't guarded around me, so he might not have realized that he was being so open without trying.

He paused momentarily, taking a thoughtful bite of his hero sandwich before returning his attention to me. I couldn't help but stare at his strong, chiseled features and think how fitting that was, feeling my face becoming flushed with embarrassment at the thought. He was, after all, my hero, saving my life more than once. "Well, we've been talking so much about the things we did as children, where you and Paige went. I thought it might be good to revisit more places from when you grew up, specifically after you moved to Bayfield. There are times when it's far easier to remember things when you have a visual cue. The sense of smell is also closely linked to memory, and so is hearing. I figured it wouldn't be the worst idea to revisit these places, although I'm sure some of them could be dangerous."

Taking a bite of my sandwich, I thought about his proposition. "Well, I mean, I've looked at a lot of places from my childhood before, and although at the time I might have gotten hazy memories or felt panicky, I never really had any huge revelations."

Luke smiled at me. "That's true, but you didn't have me around before. Now that you remember me, things have changed, and you might have a little more luck." He was right. Things were certainly different now than they were back then. I thought about it a little bit.

I smiled and looked up at him, trying to return his enthusiasm, and thought I'd try my hand at being a bit flirtatious. "So basically, you're asking if I want to go with you to these important places from our past? I mean, sounds nice to me." He smiled, though I didn't know whether or not he had picked up on the hints I was dropping. The insinuation that this was some form of romantic outing did make me feel better about it, a little less stressed, even though that almost certainly wasn't how he was thinking of it.

I was learning that Luke was in something of a state of arrested development. He was clearly a hardwired person with a lot of character and a good heart, but he had, like me, dedicated so much of his life to the single-minded pursuit of finding me. In a roundabout way, I thought we probably made a good pair—two obsessives. Probably the easiest person to relate to would be someone else with your same obsession. I couldn't help but wonder why he had chosen to come after me instead of Paige, though I hadn't raised the topic yet. Any time I brought her up, he looked pained, and I didn't want to know what he had already dug up about her, so I was leaving that conversation for another day. The fact that he didn't immediately tell me she was dead and said my search for her was important led me to believe he didn't know she was dead or something.

"Hmm. I guess that is what I'm asking you, isn't it?" He smiled at me. Maybe he had picked up on what I meant. I flushed again. "Do you have any places in mind?"

I had to think about it. We had already gone to that house in Gainesville, and now that we knew there were cult members inside the Bayfield Police Department, it was wise to avoid anywhere they would have a strong presence. That limited my options to places surrounding my childhood home, Paige's house, and our old stomping grounds. Something was calling me back to the lake where Paige and I had our many adventures with our imaginary friend. Then, there was always that persistent memory of that shapeless figure walking down the pathway that entered my mind, and I knew where we had to go.

"Do you remember that pathway that went down to the lake, the one that went through the woods? It was stunning."

Luke leaned back in his chair and looked off into the distance, clearly reminiscing. "Sure. I remember it well. The three of us used to walk down that way all the time, especially in the summer."

I nodded my head. "I think I want to go there. I have this vague recollection. Some half-formed vision that always shows up in my head, but I can never remember it clearly. I feel like I'm close though. Maybe with you there, I might be able to make some progress." Luke smiled lovingly and shrugged. "If I can be of help, then I'm happy to."

Indeed, there was already more to that memory. Until this point, I had only remembered that figure walking up and smiling, but now I remember that someone was walking beside me, or perhaps it wasn't a person, but a thing. It was an animal of some sort. Maybe a dog? I couldn't figure it out, but I knew things were changing in my head. Now, I could finally start unraveling the pieces of my past. Eager to see where it all might lead, I took a renewed interest in the lunch before me and thought to myself, "Paige, just you hold tight; I'm coming for you. Me and Luke both."

The morning was cool and crisp, typical of autumn and strangely idyllic, an odd day considering the Floridian climate. Honestly, I had never liked being in the heat and humidity of Florida, though I loved the wildlife. There was nothing as mystical and terrifying as the Everglades in my mind. On one hand, it was amazing and beautiful that there could be so much untamed wilderness on your doorstep. At the same time, it was terrifying to think that there was so much unclaimed wilderness full of dangerous animal life and a place where if you were to get lost or die, you would most likely never be found.

There was an instructor back at the police academy who liked to tell the creepy tale about how it only took a week or so for a person to be stripped down to their bones if they were left in the marshy wetlands. One would be reduced to nothing in that time due to all the insects and larger animals. It was meant to illustrate exactly how quick people needed to be in finding missing persons and murder victims, and it was also indirectly used to discourage me from my search. To me, though, it showed a flaw in our system that we thought too catastrophically if we didn't get quick results. If someone went missing in California, they'd continue the search for years, determined to find some trace. Even if a case went cold, it could be reopened at a moment's notice, but here, the red tape was too restricting.

For the longest time, I thought it was simply my own issue. The revelation that certain parties were conspiring against me truly disgusted me, but at the same time, it did put some more faith in the general policing system. Perhaps this was not the case everywhere, and just some awful twist of fate against me in particular.

It was funny to think about the Everglades as Luke and I walked down that path, because one would assume that this trail came from some other far-flung corner of the world, given its deciduous trees that sprawled up to the sky, along with its mighty oaks that were steadily changing color, even in the Florida temperatures. Under different circumstances, I imagined it would be quite a romantic outing, but with everything unfolding, there was an air of tension. I knew that we were fast approaching that place that lived so frequently in my head, and I wondered what the presence of my old friend would do to the vision.

As it turned out, I didn't need to wait long to see. Something about simply walking next to someone down this path spurred on more of that fragmented memory. There was certainly a man who had walked up the path and smiled at me, but it wasn't a stranger. I recognized the facial features, though it didn't click in my head exactly who it was. I knew I'd have to think of it for a while, but what stood out was that the animal walking next to me was not a dog, but a horse. Or no, not a horse, but, well, a beautiful white unicorn. It was my imaginary friend, Zeus. Except, this wasn't some remembrance of a game being played, but a simple walk being taken together, and I remembered him so very vividly.

19

Everywhere we visited echoed the same experience again and again. Memories would come flooding back to me, vivid pictures of my time with Paige and Luke. Most stood out, but my memory was flooded with images and shapes, and even more prevalent than I could ever have imagined, I remembered Zeus. It seemed that I could not go to a single place from my childhood without some remembrance of him as either a man or a unicorn, as I normally remembered him.

Whether seeing him in my peripheral vision or just feeling he was always nearby, I felt safe and protected in his presence. I had never known that I was so immersed in fantasy at that age, but there was also a lot of strangeness to these visions aside from his presence. Children make fanciful imaginary friends, but they're not there. They convince themselves that they are there; they imagine that they are there, but there's no actual sensory input. I could remember how Zeus smelled and how he looked, not just in my mind's eye, but rather in reality.

With the first few of these incidents, I didn't say anything to Luke, merely reporting any other memories that came to me, often commenting on how I remembered he was there at that particular location, but as we continued, and I kept getting snippets of those experiences, I realized that I needed to tell him what was happening. Of course, my primary fear was that he was going to think I was crazy. I was sure, though, that I had told him about Zeus as a child. I knew that he couldn't see him, though Paige could. That was another part of these memories that was strange.

In retrospect, Paige always knew exactly what Zeus was doing, and it always matched up entirely with how I thought of him. I had always thought to myself that the stuffed animal was what inspired my imaginary friend. But now, thinking back, I realize that many of these memories predated when I got that toy, and I believe Paige gave me the stuffed unicorn on my ninth birthday so I would never forget Zeus. Something extraordinary had happened in my childhood, and I wasn't sure how to account for it, but I knew that Luke needed my complete honesty.

We were back across the street from Harry's, where Paige, Luke, and I would always play after going to dinner there. As we walked, I couldn't help but study Luke's face. He was reminiscing, and I got the impression, as I had at so many of these places, that he hadn't been back home in a very long time. Apparently, becoming an FBI agent is a process that takes a lot of determination, and you can't decide where you're going to be, at least not at first. He hadn't opened up very much about what had happened to him since my memories of him had vanished so long ago, but I got the feeling that there was a reason why he couldn't.

Still, though, I wanted to know everything. Curiosity had always been my greatest weakness but my greatest strength. From what I had pieced together, it seemed like he had spent a fair amount of time in Virginia besides training for the FBI. His knowledge of different areas of Georgia also told me that he may have spent some time there. I realized that I was stalling in my own head, trying to keep myself from approaching an uncomfortable topic, but I had to be brave. It felt like all I did these days was confront the uncomfortable or unpleasant. Things I was starting to get pretty good at it, if I did say so myself.

"Hey, Luke . . . Do you remember my imaginary friend?" He looked thoughtfully into the tree line, pacing back and forth for a moment. He seemed to be going through his own experiences, and then suddenly, he turned toward me with his hand held up as though he had suddenly come upon a revelation.

"Oh yeah, yeah! You and Paige both had one. It was like a unicorn, right? I always thought it was kind of silly, but to be honest, it made me annoyed because it seemed like you two were sharing something I couldn't get in on, and anytime I tried to join in on the game, you always said, "No, you're not seeing it right. No, that's not what he's doing! That sort of thing pissed me off like crazy at the time." He laughed, clearly enjoying the walk down memory lane. "Why do you bring it up?" Now I felt even more self-conscious. He definitely thought of it as a game that Paige and I had played, which was to be expected, but it would have been a lot easier if he had just forgotten about it altogether and I could have informed him without any biases.

I was blushing, knowing that this would probably be the most insane thing I could bring up concerning the investigation, but it was important to explore every avenue. "Well, my imaginary friend's name was Zeus. I remember seeing him along with Paige, but the thing is, everywhere we go, I remember him. I don't mean like I remember imagining him. I mean, I literally remember being next to someone. I don't know if this is maybe a consequence of the kind of experimentation the cult did to change my memories or something like that, but I'm telling you that everywhere we go, I remember this thing. More than that, I also remember him interacting with the world in ways that an imaginary friend just couldn't."

Just like I thought, Luke looked a bit worried and confused, but he didn't outright dismiss me. "Hmm, alright. I'm not sure what that's about, but your theory that it could have something to do with where your memories have been tampered with probably holds water. I should contact the Bureau and see if any other survivors have similar incident reports." That was a relief. He was taking me seriously and didn't consider me crazy. I had some trust that he wouldn't think of me that way, but still, it was nice.

Something that became abundantly apparent the more I spent time with Luke was that he was extremely dependable. All I needed to do was say that I needed something or wanted to go somewhere or state any idea I had, and he would get on it immediately. Even in the police force, I hadn't known people so hard-working, and unlike them, he didn't complain about it.

As time passed and we continued to search places, I began to develop a sense of unease, as though we were being watched. It occurred to both of us that the creeping tendrils of the cult may extend further than we knew. According to Luke, there were at least a few hundred confirmed members. Referring to this group of people as some shapeless entity dehumanized it, but I had seen the reality of what they were. At the very least, they were human traffickers and murderers; more than that, they were disgusting and frightful to witness up close. As hard as I tried not to think about the last few weeks, my mind couldn't dismiss these sick and twisted people with some dark ambition I couldn't understand.

During my first few days with Luke, I received many phone calls from my father and the police department. I bet they were out looking for me, but I couldn't trust any of them, especially after what had happened with Rebecca. In the time since then, I had come to think clearly and realized that, in all probability, with what had happened, Cooper Harrison and perhaps even Chief Hudson were involved in the cult's agenda. It was utterly absurd, but I felt as though I was unraveling a massive conspiracy, only I wasn't someone looking at connected photos and pieces of paper on a board; I was living it. It was actively unfolding around me. As we walked on that trail, those thoughts danced in my head, replaying over and over.

I turned to Luke and, as I had gotten in the habit of doing, asked him what was weighing on my mind. "So why exactly does the cult call themselves the Disciples of the Rising Phoenix?" I was a bit surprised at myself that I hadn't asked the question before. In other circumstances, I probably would have felt embarrassed doing so, but something about being with Luke made me feel comfortable and disarmed. I knew the answer he would give me wouldn't be condescending or judgmental. He would just try to provide me with whatever information he had.

In his typical fashion, Luke shrugged, smiled at me, and scratched his head. "I don't have a good answer to that one. I have a few guesses myself, and I'm sure the boys back home have their own theories. All I can say is I know that they have some kind of plan for humanity at large, or at least they have delusions of one. I suspect the cult engages in rituals that emulate the Phoenix, a mythical golden bird dating back to ancient times. In Greek Mythology, the bird symbolized immortality and regeneration.

From what I've gathered, the cult believes there are individuals in the world who have the capacity to defeat death and transform themselves, obtaining some kind of spiritual rebirth. Who knows, maybe they're interested in eternal life, sorcery, or other stuff like that." He paused and chuckled a bit. "I mean, they do kind of look like exactly what you'd imagine a cult would, right? It's like something out of a scary story with their hooded robes, symbols, and all sorts of sketchy stuff. I guess crazy really does come in some apparent forms, huh?"

I thought for a moment. "Well, I think it's all a question of motives. Some cults are just after money, while others are trying to gain power or manipulate people. Still, I suppose that if you had a group of people who genuinely believed they had answers to the bigger questions in life, a secret knowledge, or something that could change how the world works for them, it would probably be pretty easy to make people do things that were far outside of their moral compass and to make them act in ways they would otherwise find crazy. For example, we call the robes funny, but we don't think that when we see a priest, do we? We just think that's just a part of their belief. Maybe it's the same for these guys." I turned my gaze to him, frowning. "Besides that, you can call it cheesy as much as you want, but I know just as well as you do that being up close to those guys is anything but funny. It's scary."

We walked in silence for a little bit, both of us thinking about the close encounters we had had. Looking at Luke, I could tell he had something to say, but he wasn't always the best at being the one to initiate. I decided I would wait until he had worked up the nerve or found the words he was looking for. My patience paid off after a few minutes when he turned to me with a look of embarrassment and perhaps a bit of fear. "There is something I've been wanting to ask you about, Olivia. Not about our past, but more recently at that house. Am I the only one who thought the last guy we saw, you know, the one who didn't go down after getting shot, looked wrong? Am I right?" I nodded my head, vividly remembering the strange colossal figure. "I hope you won't think badly of me for this, Olivia, but I think about that guy a lot. Lately, I've been finding it kind of hard to sleep because I see his face, or, well, I guess not really the face, but staring at those eyes just feels wrong." I knew exactly how he felt.

We kept walking. My head was turned down, and I was thinking about his words, going over them. I knew I wasn't insane, and I didn't think he was either, but the implications of what we had seen at that house were scarring. It made me feel unsafe. I wished that I was somewhere, anywhere else. I must have seemed pretty miserable because I felt my hand suddenly get squeezed, not hard, just reassuringly, and looking over, I saw that Luke had reached out to hold my hand. I almost pulled my hand away as a force of nervous habit, but I stopped myself, thinking a moment. I wrapped my fingers around his and turned to him, smiling; we both may have been scared, but being together made things feel better.

It hadn't been that long since the morning with Rebecca had happened, only about a month, but once I had regained my memories, there were years of experience that I had shared with this man. Of course, that was back when we were both little, but I knew him, and I trusted him. Deep down, I knew that I was falling in love with him, or maybe I already had when we embraced in the hotel, but with everything else that had just happened, I had pushed the thought away, not wanting to admit it to myself yet. I knew I would soon have to because those feelings were growing by the day. I wasn't that worried, though, because it seemed like he shared them. At least I hoped he did.

Suddenly, I was snapped back from this fuzzy romantic haze by an acute awareness that something was wrong. Looking in front of me, I immediately identified it. It was as though history was repeating itself. A lone figure was walking up the path toward us, grinning. He wore a black overcoat and dressed far heavier than needed. A wide-brimmed hat covered his head. To say that he looked conspicuous would be an understatement. No, the more accurate description would be that this man looked extremely strange. He was also lanky and quite tall, but more characteristic than any of this was his grin, slightly too wide. His eyes, I recognized, weren't exactly the same, but of the same type as the man in the house, with that twinkling searchlight gaze. My blood ran cold in my veins.

20

In broad daylight, there was no confusion of dim lighting or the idea that my eyes were playing tricks on me. It was obvious to me that there was something very wrong with this man. He had the look of someone crazed, but even worse, the look of someone who was fundamentally flawed, as though some small part of his humanity had dissolved. Instinctively, I reached for my holster, and I could tell that Luke was doing the same as he tore his hand away from mine.

Before either one of us could reach our pieces, however, the man put his hands up. It wasn't a sign of surrender but a form of mockery as his mouth distorted into a grimacing smile. "Don't be so hasty now. I'm not here to attack you." His voice was deep and raspy, as though he had smoked for most of his life. The man looked toward me, his piercing gaze running over me and seemingly penetrating my head.

"Olivia, there are a lot of people who are worried about you. You really should go and check in with them. Think about how Cooper's feeling, or your father, for that matter." His mocking grin widened.

I was too afraid to speak. Thankfully, Luke was already shouting. "Keep your hands where I can see them, and don't make any sudden movements!" His gun was already drawn, but the strange man seemed utterly unconcerned and unthreatened, turning his face toward Luke. Looking at the man's expression was nauseating. I couldn't place it exactly, but there was something so familiar about him, not only the figure I had seen in the dilapidated house among the cultists, but also something that came from my past that my mind continued to block.

His eyes continued to stare into mine. Still, he refused to acknowledge Luke even as he shouted commands. "Remember, Olivia, we're always watching. You're never too far away from safety or from those who care about you. When your little rebellious phase ends, we will welcome you with open arms. Don't worry too much about what's happened. We don't hold it against you." His patronizing tone carried a moral wrongness laced with unequivocal hatred. It was like he was sneering at me with nothing but his inflections. Still, underneath that inhuman and disgusting nature, he had a strange yet loving affection to his expression that made my skin crawl.

I felt my blood boiling, "Welcome me back? I don't even know who your people are, let alone why you're so obsessed with me. Why don't you all just leave me alone?" It was the first time I had actually been able to talk to someone who had brazenly presented themselves as part of this faceless force that called themselves the Disciples of the Rising Phoenix. I think it was understandable that I had anger I wished to express. It was my right to be angry, just as much as it was my right to get answers!

These people had played with my life and my destiny for most of what I had known. They had taken what was important to me in more ways than one and traumatized me beyond repair. I wanted to shoot this man. If truth be told, I wanted to shoot any one of these freaks that I ran into. I was stopped in this bloody line of thought by the faces I knew from my childhood and everyday life, those who had shown me love and affection and had helped me. Surely they weren't simple monsters. Those feelings were real, weren't they? The whole thing made me feel nauseous.

The man's hands were still up. Luke had stopped shouting orders, instead keeping his pistol trained on the uncanny stranger's head. Logically, I knew I was safe with a trained marksman aiming at him, but I didn't feel safe. For some reason that I can't explain, I felt that nothing he could do would stop this man if he decided to hurt us, not even bullets. The man in the hat wasn't smiling anymore, and that allowed me a better look at his features when they weren't twisted into a grimace.

It was no more pleasant without the unsettling expression; still, the mouth was too wide. Now, without the wrinkles of the smile covering it up, I could see an irregularity to the skin on his face, as though it was unnaturally aged or even perhaps scaly in certain places. Not only that, but its color was slightly off. He was not quite Caucasian, but his skin tone was more grayish, reflecting a dull, faded, and ashy look. It was difficult to figure out what expression he was using while staring at his strange face. The smile was so overblown that it was recognizable even in its warped state, but it was difficult to determine without that expression. What was going on in this man's mind? It almost felt as if I was witnessing a disappointment in that tightlipped, drawn expression.

"We can't leave you alone, Olivia. Just as we can't leave anyone alone who has the probability to be a candidate." For just a moment, he shot an extremely venomous glance toward Luke. "You may think of our methods as disturbing or our nature as unnatural. I can understand this view from an unenlightened one. I assure you, though, that our goals are all dedicated to the greater good, and I have to say that I'm disappointed that you have not yet understood what our motives are. Your father would be very disappointed, Olivia." Again, a strange sense of familiarity crept over me. I didn't know where, but I recognized this voice from somewhere. Or maybe that wasn't it. It wasn't that I recognized his voice, because the inflection of his voice was different, but the tempo of his speech was very similar. It was like hearing a familiar song sung in a different key.

I couldn't hold in my curiosity. I was fixated on the man's voice, on why it would sound familiar. There was the beginning of a half-formed memory in my head. "I know you." My voice was shaky; of that fact, I was sure. I definitely knew this person, though the face was alien; this thing was linked to my past. This familiarity sent chills down my spine. I felt like I was once again teetering on the edge of something large and trying to brace myself for it.

The malformed stranger again shifted expressions. Now, he was frowning, and there was a lot more distinction to this mask. This sadness appeared subdued in comparison to his distorted smile the moment before. Still, though, there was some inherent feeling of wrongness to it, and his eyes still spoke of a condescending sneer. "You're telling me that you don't remember? But we had such good times together. It wasn't this trail, but another very much like it. Leading up to that shining blue-green water. I remember that the birds were singing that day." My head felt like it was going to explode.

A searing memory shot through me, and suddenly, pieces that had not been connected, pieces blocked out by trauma, reignited my mind to create a complete picture where there had only been excerpts and a sense of unease before. The man before me looked nothing like I remembered, but I recalled the voice. It was softer back then, far softer and kinder. I had remembered him so many times, walking up to me on the trail leading to the lake. I could never remember his face. It was always clouded like the police officer's face had been. Now, in my memory, I knew why, for they were one and the same, and not only that, but memories of this man extended further back than seeing him at that lake trail.

How could it be? The man, I recall, was already past his prime. I would have thought in his fifties, which would now mean he would be in his seventies or maybe even eighties, but he didn't look it. He barely even looked human, but aside from that, there was no way he could have looked that much younger. My eyes scanned the monstrous man for some kind of clue, some indication as to what had happened and what he exactly was, but I found nothing other than more disturbing details in that uncanny face. I could not look at it for much longer, so I averted my eyes, but already he had realized the change in my demeanor.

"Ah, yes, Olivia, I see it on your face; there dawns understanding! I'm simply overjoyed that you remember me. At the time, I went by the name of Decker, and as you may remember, I worked for the police at the time." What he was saying was true. I remembered it. I even remembered my dad referencing "Officer Decker" on several occasions, other times referring to him as "Deck" when off duty. What truly worried me was that I had memories of that man I had never pieced together before, which came before I moved to Florida. I eyed him suspiciously and felt that he could pick up on my unspoken question. "You have a better memory than I would have imagined, Olivia. I see the recognition in your eyes. I know that you remember me from before you came to Bayfield. It's good that you do. It makes things so much easier. You could say that it was I, along with your father, who scouted your talent originally back when you were with poor Camila." The hideous thing grimaced.

There were no words for what I was hearing. It was becoming too much to process. I found myself retreating into a dark place with the overwhelming information I was preparing to hear and receive a revelation upon. However . . . I wasn't prepared to hear about my mother.

21

"What the hell did you do to my mother, you freak?"

I spat the words out like venom. There was so much hatred welling up inside me that I could not keep a reasonable or objective tone. I could feel my hand squeezing the grip of my pistol. I wanted more than anything to shoot this man dead; it was not self-defense, and I knew that, but still, my passion flared up inside, and I was so dangerously close to doing it.

"If I told you, would that make you want to come with me? Is that the carrot that I need to offer you?" Again, the voice was full of condescension, and once more, that twisted smile had broken across his menacing face. "Do you know what your issue is, girl? You're too selfish! It's always about something concerning you, never about others, never about what's happening around you in the world or how you could help. No, no, if it's not in your little personal crusade, then you have no interest at all, do you? What would poor Paige think of that?"

Something started to snap inside me, and I knew I was drawing my gun, but it was as though I was in a dreamlike state of altered consciousness. I wasn't adequately processing what I was doing. It was simply on instinct; however, I hadn't cleared the leather of my holster before a splitting sound rang out, and I knew a shot had already been fired, not from me, but from Luke. He had cut the thing off mid-sentence by shooting it in the temple. In less than a moment, I realized what I was doing and knew I had been close to murdering this monstrous thing.

I looked over at Luke; his face was of grim determination, but something in it spoke of compassion. I think I knew what he was thinking, that he was already a killer, and as much as I loved him, that fact was unshakeable. I had shot someone in self-defense in a life-or-death scenario, but I had never reached this point. I guessed that Luke had already crossed that line long ago. I wanted to think his actions were justified and he wanted to protect what vital parts of me and my innocence remained.

The man slumped as soon as the shot rang out, hitting the ground with heavy force. I heard the crack of his skull before the spattering of blood reached me. The air of the place changed. No longer was it a tense confrontation; rather, there was an unmistakable sense of anger. Directed from what, I didn't know, but it was certainly there. I did not need to wait long to figure it out. As soon as the body bled out on the pavement, more of the figures, some robed, some in crude streetwear attempting to cover up their malformed bodies and faces, seemingly appeared from nowhere. I realized now why the man hadn't cared about the threat of violence from Luke. He hadn't come on his own, and it was foolish to think he had.

My handgun was drawn as I fell back with Luke, trying to squeeze into a tight formation where we could cover each other. I counted at least eight of them, though I sensed more lurking off the path in those woods. I was waiting for them to come at us. We were so outnumbered that even if they had knives, they could carve us to pieces. The rush never came though; instead, they all looked at me as they went and leaned over their fallen comrade, and then I heard a terrible, unnatural sound. It was a sucking wheeze as if someone's lungs had collapsed and they were trying desperately to get air inside; however, it was worse than that. It wasn't just strange breathing. There was a rhythm to it, a pulse and a grave tone that told me that what I was hearing was some hideous, completely depraved form of laughter.

What truly made it detestable, though, was where this laughter was coming from. It was not from the trail's edge nor any of the robed figures on the path, but from the thing with a bullet in its head. My hearing was not wrong because even as I looked, the figure began to sit up. The twisted smile was still on his face, his beady eyes intense and terrifying, seemingly not bothered by the blood trickling down his skull. What I was looking at went beyond strange. It went beyond gruesome. It crossed into a realm of impossibility so absolute and terrible that I could not process it.

How I wish I could relate my heroic escape. I wish that I could tell you about how I bravely faced off against the cultists, how I fled in victory. I wish I could even say that it was a tactical retreat. In reality, though, the memories are fuzzy. I recall screaming and nearly collapsing to my knees. I remember Luke grabbing my wrist and wrenching me, sprinting out. I remember their strange laughter, childlike but berating, and I remember the unmistakable feeling that we were being let go. I still didn't know for what reason, but the wheels were still spinning inside of my head, and I knew that my answers would come to me. My sense of reality had been thoroughly rocked, causing the processes of my brain to act in ways I had never allowed before. My thoughts had always been constrained by some form of normalcy that ruled everyday life, but now I realized that what I was witnessing as reality was, at least in part, a lie.

I remember very little about the escape. I know I was thankful to Luke for taking that shot and pulling me away from those creatures. I don't know how we got back to the car, where we sped off to, or how we tried to escape. I don't even remember how we got our belongings from the motel before we started leaving. A solid train of thought resurfaced as I replayed the gruesome scene in my head. I imagine it would now seem exceedingly foolish after an hour of driving in silence down the interstate. Still, at the time, I wasn't thinking with much clarity, so, somewhat dreamily, my first question was simply, "Where are we going?"

I was fortunate that the person I was with was Luke. Someone else might have poked fun at me or taken their own stresses and turned them into anger, using me as a punching bag. He was not only receptive to my moods but always seemed to be understanding of my situation. He looked at me, somewhat worried, clearly aware of my mental state, and simply said, "I'm not sure. Faraway, I guess."

I looked at the situation and regarded my life up until this point, hearing that simplified answer. That it so concisely put together what needed to be done, without any of the reasoning I would have tried to present it with, was, for some reason, hilarious. I couldn't help but laugh. It wasn't a hysterical laugh or the result of terror dawning on me, but genuine laughter that came from understanding someone trying to do their best in a situation that was far beyond them. By some miracle, I relaxed back in my seat and looked out on the road. Maybe I was running from reality and what had happened, and if I was, that was probably for the best.

There were no ifs, ands, or buts about it. I knew that for a slight moment back there, I had lost my mind, teetering on the edge of insanity. The fact that the same thing hadn't happened to Luke astonished me and told me so much about his character. At some point, we would need to discuss it and figure out what we thought was going on, but that time certainly wasn't now. Seconds passed into minutes, and I thought of what to say next. Eventually, I decided I was too tired for formality and too tired to consider the right thing to say, so I decided to just say what came to mind.

"You know, Luke, I'm not sure what the government pays you or what kind of budget you have, but if we have to flee for our safety, do you think there's any chance we could go somewhere scenic and quiet? I don't know about you, but I could use a break from all of what's happening." I knew it was a silly request and entirely unreasonable to boot, but I also thought that he might want to get away too. Our situation needed some tranquility and a dose of light humor to break up the oppressive amount of sadness and terror that pursued us. I looked over and saw a genuinely thoughtful expression on his face. I wondered if he was trying to think of how to let me down gently or if he was thinking of some way to make my request come true. It's not as if I really wanted to run away from reality or what was happening, but I knew that to regain my memories, I needed peace and quiet, and it seemed that anywhere we were, I couldn't find that. What was necessary right now was a home base and some form of safe house.

"Unfortunately, Olivia, I'm not paid too much. I make a comfortable living wage, but certainly not while I'm out on assignment, and I'm not given an unlimited budget to do what I need to when I am out in the field, but I actually might have an idea." I cocked a brow questioningly as he looked at me with a wolfish grin. "You know, I feel bad. All this time, we've been going back to places that were either tough for you or important to you, but other than the places we shared from childhood, I haven't been able to show you anything of mine. Maybe I can change that now. Back when I first had to go into witness protection, there was a place where we stayed. It was kind of like a camp. It's a cabin on the water. I know that I could get access to it, and it would definitely be safe there." He laughed and looked over to me, extending a hand and squeezing mine. I took comfort from the gesture.

"You know, maybe it's just because I feel like we cheated death, but I'm a little excited at the prospect of showing something of mine to you, especially considering how vulnerable you've had to be with me. I'm sorry about how hard this past month's been. It's never been my intention to bring you misery; in fact, I wanted to put an end to it." What could I possibly say to that? That I didn't blame him? It was true, I didn't, but I got the feeling that Luke was the type that took this sort of responsibility onto himself. I could say, though, that my feelings for him took me by surprise. Finding out who he was and remembering the fun times together from our childhood, coupled with all of the time getting to personally know him in the past month, I could look back on and smile. What could I say to him to put his mind at ease? To let him know that I didn't think of him as an enemy?

I racked my brain looking for the right words, going over and over again, thinking back to the times I could recall Paige and I playing at our make-believe castle with Zeus, waiting for our prince to sweep us off our feet while he battled the evil villain. It was our happily ever after; only now, my prince had come to life in Luke. The number of times he had saved me from God knows what those things were, he was, in every way, my hero. I couldn't stop thinking of the times that we shared lunches in the motel, laughing at the funny yet far-fetched stories of our childhood adventures, and at the same time feeling the sexual chemistry that was growing between us. From how he looked at me, I knew we both felt its overwhelming power surging like electric shock sensations that could light up an entire room.

At that moment, I wanted to throw my arms around him and feverishly kiss him to show him how I felt. It may have been the acts of heroism, it may have been the adrenaline, it may have been any number of things, but all I could really think to do was say one thing. I squeezed his hand tighter as his look changed to that of worry, perhaps thinking I was going back into a state of shock. Instead, his eyes met mine as I whispered, "Luke, I love you."

22

The circumstances were all wrong, and I knew that. I realized, though, that the reality of what was happening was that we were on the run from a cult, one that possessed inhuman powers and was involved in the deaths and abductions of many people, many of whom were children. Still, I had never had any time for affection or love in my life, and the rest of that ride had been unlike anything else I had ever experienced. Despite my worries, he had felt the same way, and apparently, he had felt that way since we were little and it was a contributing factor to why he had spent so much time and effort tracking me down. I thought it was crazy that anyone would go to that length of trouble for my sake, but that only made my affection stronger for him.

Despite these terrible circumstances, when we arrived at a beautiful lakeside cabin nestled in a secluded woodland, I felt almost like it was a romantic getaway. Of course, part of me knew that I was thinking this way because of the excitement of the ride over, and another part of it was most likely a coping mechanism to try to deal with the horror I had witnessed only hours beforehand. Right now, though, I didn't want to think about it. I had spent so much time over this past period of my life confronting horror, always having to press on, and for once, I welcomed the opportunity to step away from it and simply enjoy the moment. Sometimes, the soul should run far, far away, to a place of peace and solitude.

I genuinely believe that. If one faces every harsh reality, one after another, again and again, it will wear down one's moral compass. Not only will it do that, but also it will corrupt one's sense of self. Eventually, you will end up as a broken, barely functional person. The same could be said for any strong conviction not diluted by the world around you. That is why we find things we enjoy, such as hobbies, friends, lovers, or any number of things that will take our minds away from the hard parts of reality that we often need to confront. This is not weakness. It is how we regain the strength and courage to go back again and fight for what we believe in. That's what I was telling myself as I walked into that cabin.

It was lovely and furnished rustically. I had only seen interior decoration and architecture like it in turn-of-the-century cabins displayed in magazines or on television. Certainly, I had never stayed in a place like it. Luke brought our bags to the middle of the room, dropping them down and gesturing to his surroundings with a beaming grin. "Well, I guess you could say this is my place. I did live here for a few years, and I still like to come back when I want to clear my head." Suddenly, he got an expression on his face like something was weighing on him. "Maybe I should have just brought us here to begin with. I don't know why it didn't occur to me, but . . ." He trailed off, clearly lost in his own thoughts.

I knew that he was thinking about how he could have better protected me and kept me from as much pain as possible, but that simply wasn't an option. I wasn't going to let him torture himself, so I came to the center of the room and sat on the couch next to him, putting my hand on his cheek and turning his face toward me, summoning up the warmest smile I could.

"Don't beat yourself up about it. Don't you remember we needed to go to places from our childhood to try to jog memories? I couldn't have done that here. We would have had to be in Gainesville for it. Plus, with how I thought of you, do you really think you could have convinced me to come to your place?" Maybe I had worded that wrong. As the implications of what I had just said washed over Luke, he suddenly turned beat red.

The flustered agent stumbled over his words as he tried to answer, "W-well, no, I didn't mean it like that. I just, well . . ." I had never seen him so flustered, and to think it was just because of me was odd but certainly pleasant. He was cute when he was flustered. I wanted to hold on to this, to this feeling of warmth and kindness, this happiness. I knew what was coming would be terrible, and I would have to face more pieces of myself that I'd never wanted to surface again. I also knew that our future loomed with those horrible figures in robes, barely human and able to withstand more abuse than anyone could. How I wished I could just hang on to this feeling forever, this lovely yet uncharted euphoria.

"I'm joking, you big dummy! I know you didn't mean it like that." He was so damn earnest in trying to defend himself and his actions even when he wasn't doing anything wrong. That sincere and intense conviction made him so difficult to be angry at, even at the worst of times. He was still very obviously embarrassed, but less so. Why did I suddenly feel like my heart would jump through my chest? My jokes had only masked my nervousness, keeping my arousing anxiety at bay. Here I was, at the house of the man I had fallen in love with, and I had to admit, I didn't want what I was feeling to end. I wanted to learn more about him and to be in safety and privacy for as long as was necessary. I wasn't planning to abandon what I was doing at all, but it would be a complete fabrication to say that I had no plans to enjoy this moment in time.

Luke got back to his feet and helped me up next to him. "Let me show you around. I've used this place so many times that I know it like the back of my hand, and I may or may not have made some minor alterations to the cabin myself." As it turns out, those minor alterations were fairly major; a lot of it had been built by him and his father. It was an interesting mixture of a comfortable cabin and a place that agents would use at the Bureau. On one hand, there was a lovely den decorated in a charming, old-fashioned style. On the other was a basement full of weaponry and loading benches. It was an interesting blend of practicality and functionality, and I found it quite charming. I thought the house was a good reflection of Luke as a man.

The lake outside was beautiful, brimming with an abundant population of rainbow trout and a fair number of other fish that called these waters their home. According to Luke, each spring, you could see the turtles nest and watch their babies being born if you had the right viewpoint. He also warned me that it wasn't uncommon for porcupines or black bears to wander into the area around the cabin. I loved it. I had never had too many opportunities to go out into nature. I was so absorbed in my goals that I had seen the years I would have gone to summer camp fly by studying or training.

The whole thing to me seemed so novel and idyllic. I must have seemed a little too happy because Luke had to reiterate harshly that the black bears were something to worry about and that if I saw one, I really shouldn't get close but rather either get him or lock the doors. I wanted to say that I could handle myself, but I've never really been in the wilderness other than back when I was a child, so, truth be told, I didn't know how to deal with black bears.

Still, it was undeniable how pleasant it was to talk to him about these things. Ever since we had met, it was always a matter of dire consequence and importance. I had had precious little time, aside from our meals together and those rare days where we had nothing happening, where I got to see the man that Luke was outside of his role, helping me, and I was enthralled by what I was seeing. It was as if all the positive traits I had remembered in him as a boy had flourished and taken root, turning him into a resourceful and loving man.

I was impressed by his patience with someone like me who had never been in a situation like this before. Aside from that, he clearly put so much care into the area's upkeep. It's a bit of a silly thing to say, but I've always been a sucker for guys who are handyman types and know how to do things on their own without help. So, the fact that he built half of the sizable cabin was quite captivating.

At the end of his little grand tour, Luke led me up toward the rooms. Part of me was disappointed to figure out that he had gotten a guest room ready for me, and a small piece of me was hoping we would end up sharing the master bedroom, but another part of me was relieved. That was another awkward part of myself I wouldn't have to face right now, at least not until I was ready, and I appreciated that he hadn't made any assumptions. It was a lovely room, and I liked the cottage-style bed. Only after I set foot in the room did I realize how tired I was now that all of the adrenaline was wearing off. I was utterly exhausted. Luke said that tomorrow would be a good day to go into town and surprised me with the suggestion that we could go shop for clothes since I hadn't brought very much in the luggage we were able to grab from the motel.

I nodded. It was a nice idea, and I was excited to get out for a bit. With nothing else to do, I lay down in bed, turned off the light, and waited for sleep to take over. Despite how tired I was, it was extremely difficult to get rest. My mind was still racing with everything that had happened, but more than anything, I thought back to what that beast that called itself Decker had said. It implied it knew my mother, and it called her by name. Her gentle caress and lullabies replayed repeatedly in my head, but now more was coming. Just as I had that morning, I knew that my mind was starting to fill in gaps that I had never dreamed would be filled. My memory, far from being spotty, was starting to become photographic, and the details of that memory were almost too much to bear.

23

I couldn't say when sleep finally took over, but I passed out and slept like a baby when it did.

The morning came quickly. I was accustomed to waking up in a dark room with curtains drawn, being shifted into awareness by an alarm, but this was different. I was rising as the sun was. It was pleasant and gentle, and part of what rocked me back into consciousness was not only the natural lighting but the soft song of birds outside. I don't think I had ever felt so refreshed after a night's sleep, even as troubled as I was to get there. It took me a few moments to recall my circumstances and why I was in this beautiful stately room, but once I had, I went through a bewildering array of mixed emotions once again. Fear, disgust, terror, rage, and then, that happiness and anxious affection from the previous night. I checked the bedside clock to see what time it was, finding that it was earlier than I had expected, only about seven o'clock in the morning.

Finding that I was in no rush, I stretched and lay back in the bed, replaying what I was thinking. Inevitably, I found my mind drifting back to memories of my mother, Camila. As far as I had ever known, she died when I was little, and not soon after, my father and I moved to Bayfield. What I remembered then did not fit that story, and it only made my memories that still existed a hazy, jumbled mess.

Perhaps the most pressing and distressing of all these emerging early childhood memories, from a practical standpoint, was my father's absence. For the life of me, I couldn't remember him until we needed to move. I do remember a fatherly figure, a paternal set of eyes watching over me. I remember it being jovial and loving, but what I had always thought of as my dad before my mother's death wasn't completely clear in my mind. It was someone else. I was always under the impression that I simply hadn't remembered my mother's decline.

Children don't always remember seeing their parents in pain or sickness. It can be so painful that the mind tends to block it out, but there was no sign of decline whatsoever in my memories. In fact, up until my last memories of her, she was loving and energetic. Also, as a terrible confirmation of what I already knew, I only had memories after the move of being called the name that I recognized myself by. Before that, I remember being called "the little Harper girl." This was only the worst of it from a practical standpoint. If I was allowing myself to think in the more abstract, there were far more distressing memories.

One day in particular stood out to me like nothing else. It was a rainy day, and I had gone out to play in the puddles. Back in Gainesville, we lived near a field. I think it was when I was four or five. There was a magnificent old oak tree in the middle of that field, and I went near it. I remember being with my mom, and just as we were walking through, lightning struck the tree. I was so scared. I had never seen lightning, certainly not that close, though I had heard thunder. I cried out to my mom, and she comforted me. She didn't know what I was crying about and thought I was afraid of the lightning. She told me that lightning came from up above and that it wasn't a bad thing at all.

She was such an intelligent woman but mostly lived in a consciousness of fairy tales and myths. She consoled me by telling me the old myths of the creatures and gods that people thought were responsible for thunder, and that's when she told me about Zeus, a god of lightning or thunder that the Greeks worshipped. They thought he was a protector of humanity, which put my mind at ease. At the time, I couldn't articulate what I had seen because I wasn't crying because of the lightning. I was scared because, in that lightning, I had seen a silhouette, something like a man or an animal, that flashed on the tree. That was the first time I saw who I thought of as my imaginary friend, whom I called Zeus.

Whatever Zeus was, I think that he recognized that I could see or feel him because ever since that day, I saw him more and more frequently. Sometimes, he was like a man, or not quite, but a humanoid silhouette. Other times, he appeared as a great white steed with a horn. I was too young to know what a unicorn was or connect it with the fairy tales I had been told, so at the time, I always just called it the white horsey. My poor mom didn't understand what I was talking about and just thought I wanted to hear more about unicorns. Of course, one transitioned into the other.

As a child, I loved fairy tales and quickly associated them with magical places filled with danger, new experiences, and love. Before too long, I saw Zeus almost daily and played games with him in the woods. Sometimes, I'd go on walks, and there would be a tree blocking my path, or maybe I'd want to climb up on the rocks but couldn't do it. He'd always catch me and pull me up or move the tree for me. I remember thinking that he was always so helpful. I felt safe with him. I never even considered how strange it was. That's part of being a child, I suppose. You don't know what's real and what isn't yet, and because of that, you can accept the strange as you would the normal. My "imaginary friend" was as normal a part of life as anything else.

Perhaps because of that same childish instinct that what I saw must be normal or commonplace, I didn't keep my lips closed about him. No, I told everyone who would listen about my pal the unicorn. Maybe that wouldn't have been a problem if I had lived in a different area or near different people, but before I knew it, I started seeing certain people who heard about it more frequently. First slowly and then more. Many times, it would be out on my walks when I was playing that I would notice some men walking along. Sometimes, certain women from the town would come by and talk to my mom, only I didn't remember them being friends before. I remembered that Mom had a certain friend who was always coming by, and my Dad didn't like him. But Mom thought he was nice to have around, especially because he kept an eye on me. His name was Todd Decker, a local policeman.

My skin crawled, and my stomach was sour. It was my fault. Everything that had happened, whatever had happened to my mom, had most likely happened to Paige. I was so little and loved sharing stories about Zeus with anyone who would listen. I couldn't keep my mouth shut, and people took notice that I wasn't just a girl with an imaginary friend. People started to notice something else going on, and even then, if I had been more secretive in my play sessions with whatever Zeus was, maybe they would have just thought it was my imagination. Being followed on the trails and around town proved that there was something physical happening.

At that time, I must have become a target for the cult. One other person came around perhaps even more often than Todd Decker though. I didn't like him too much at the time, and everyone else found him a gloomy, anxious sort of person. He was a respected member of the community, and at the time, he also worked for the police department, though I never would have known it, as he usually was in plain clothes. Of all of these people who had shown up, who

I now recognized as members of the cult, he was the one who had eyes on me the most. He was the one that scared me even when I was small. His name was Simon Monroe. I wanted to cry remembering that.

There were still things that didn't add up and that I didn't know. How had I ended up with Simon, and what had happened to my mother and father? What had happened to Paige? There were even a lot of questions that I still had regarding Luke. I knew that now was the time to ask them. We had privacy, and we had time. This was where I would make my stand internally. I would get to the bottom of all my burning questions. Something still was nagging at me aside from those though.

I wondered to myself what had happened to Zeus. I hadn't seen him after Paige's disappearance, or maybe it was just that he hadn't come around anymore. But why? What had happened? I knew there was still a piece of the puzzle missing, but it was one I would need to uncover to figure out exactly what had happened and regain my lost connections. I needed to understand what this creature was that had followed me throughout my life and what connection it had to the cult. I understood now that they only started trailing me after they found out I could see it so clearly, and it had to do with whoever their "candidates" were.

Other than that, though, all I could do was guess. Clearly, they had stumbled upon something aside from normal reality. They were different than normal people; at least some of them were like Luke had said. The Disciples of the Rising

Phoenix might believe in some sort of spiritual rebirth. Perhaps they thought that this creature was somehow a key to immortality. Worse, perhaps, they thought he could be used to raise the dead from their graves. There wasn't much to go on, and I had no idea how close I was to the truth, but it was a working theory, and having a theory gave me some comfort, no matter how absurd it might be.

There also remained the question of why I could see Zeus when others couldn't. Why were there candidates, and what exactly did it mean to be one? What would they groom people into once they found out they could see creatures like this? Or maybe there was only one creature to see? Again, I felt a sense of unease and fear creep over me. I had been lucky and gotten to where I was, somewhat safe if not confused and distressed, but what of the other candidates? Luke said that at least some of them were dead. What did that mean for Paige, then?

For the first time in a couple of weeks, my thoughts drifted back to detective Rebecca Roan. How had she come to work for the cult and been brought to such a state of violence? That wasn't just the actions of someone drawn in by a conspiracy theory, but of someone with absolute and utter conviction. It dawned on me that she may have been one of these candidates. How had they altered her memories? How had they changed how she thought? Was she the hero of her own story, and was she ultimately a victim? It was becoming increasingly clear to me that that may have been exactly the case, and I felt grief well up in my chest. There was nothing I could have done to save her from what had already been done, but that didn't mean I couldn't live to avenge the friend I had made.

I looked back toward the clock. Not much time had passed. Now it was only seven thirty. I didn't think I could keep replaying these memories in my head. It was now time to get up and face the day.

24

My body was stiff from the previous night. As nice as the bed was, it was still unfamiliar, and I found aches and pains that I knew I would have until I got used to the sleeping arrangement. I decided it would be best to shower before getting ready. The hot water would do me good, especially after all the stresses of the previous day.

After doing my best to scrub off all the fatigue and mental anguish I could, I got out and dried off. By this point, I realized that there was an enticing smell coming from downstairs, so I hurriedly dressed and headed down to see what was cooking. In the time we had spent at the motel, there weren't any kitchen appliances, so we had primarily eaten out, but even then, I could tell it was disappointing for Luke. On several occasions, he had said he wished he could show me his cooking, and I had become somewhat eager to try it.

Walking into the kitchen, I was somewhat taken off guard. I had only known Luke Hayes to wear suits—he was always dressed for his job—so it was somewhat strange to see him in casual clothing. He was wearing a plain T-shirt and an open flannel on top of it. As embarrassing as it is to say, one of the first things I noticed was that it was a lot more flattering than the suit; although he looked great in the suit, it was just that I had seen him in it so often that I had come to expect it. His sleeves were rolled up for cooking, and I could see his muscular forearms. The slightly sheer shirt also showed that he was well-toned and had trained extensively, which one would expect for an FBI agent, but it wasn't always noticeable in the thicker clothing he wore on the job. Somewhat consciously, I realized I was blushing and looked away.

Luke had already noticed me watching and turned back to me with a bright smile on his face. "Good morning. I don't know if you remember what I said, but back in the motel, I promised I'd cook for us when I had the chance." As he looked at me, his smile faded as he cocked his head to the side. "Are you alright?"

I didn't know how to respond to that question. I couldn't say I was staring at him admiringly, so I just nodded. Then I realized what he meant. It was quite colder in the cabin than I was used to down in Florida, and I suppose I was shivering. Before I could say anything, he had already taken off the flannel and tossed it to me. I put it on, and it was huge, but at least it was warm. Now Luke was just in a T-shirt. I had no idea how he could be comfortable given the temperature, but I wasn't about to complain.

"Thanks. I appreciate it." I realized that I still didn't know where we were. I hadn't thought to ask that last night. I was feeling self-conscious and a bit silly. Here I was, a detective, and I hadn't even thought to verify our location. If anything, that could be a testament to exactly how stressful the previous day had been. All I knew was that we had driven for hours, probably close to twelve. If we hadn't started the journey so early in the day, we certainly would have hit this place by nightfall. I swallowed my pride and decided that I had to ask. "Uh, Luke. Where exactly, well, where are we?" Luke looked at me strangely.

"I guess I didn't really say where we were headed, just that we were going to this cabin. That's my bad. I'm sorry about that, Olivia. We're right on the border of Pennsylvania now." I was a bit stunned; however, given the emotional distress I was in from what had taken place, I wasn't surprised. I believed some part of me didn't want to know where we were. I had always thought of Pennsylvania as nearly across the country. To think that we had driven all that way through the day was shocking, but then again, I didn't travel much, and of course, my mind was a mangled mess.

As I considered the information, he picked up a skillet and put eggs onto a plate. There was also toast, bacon, and pancakes with homemade maple syrup. It looked like Luke had outdone himself. With a little flush of embarrassment and excitement, I wondered if he was trying to impress me.

Whatever the case was, it looked delicious, and I was hungry. I hadn't eaten anything the previous day and hadn't felt like it, but now, with safety, I felt a voracious appetite rearing its head.

After breakfast, Luke invited me onto the patio to see the lake. It was still early enough to see mist coming off the water, and it was beautiful to witness. Every now and then, a bird of prey would swoop down, grabbing a fish from the placid lake surface. For so much of our time together, we had talked about my history and past. I wanted to learn more about him that day, so as we were sitting there just watching nature, I asked, "It must have been difficult going from Florida to this?" I looked over at him; his face was still calm, and he kept his stare out onto the lake as he considered the statement, taking a sip from his coffee.

"Well, it was different, but I can't say that I regret what I did. Having to run was hard, not only for me but for my family, and I regret putting them through that, but when I think of the alternative, I don't think that I could look back on the decision with anything but pride." It seemed that I had somewhat caught him off guard. He hadn't told me exactly why he had ever needed to run away. I could assume it had to do with what had happened with Paige and myself. Certainly, it had to do with the cult, but I hadn't gotten all of the story.

"What exactly happened to you, Luke?" All at once, Luke seemed to remember that I didn't know the details of what he was talking about, and his expression turned sour. Suddenly, he seemed far more self-conscious; even the smallest spark of distress or anger was in his face.

"I wish I could say otherwise, Olivia, but I don't want to discuss it." There was no room for argument in the tone of his voice, though I was disappointed. I had bared my soul to him many times, and hearing that he couldn't trust me with this made me feel bad. At the same time, I recognized that everyone relates their trauma differently and that just because I was ready to share what had happened didn't mean he was. It was also possible that his story had painful elements I had no inkling of.

Perhaps it would be best if I dropped it for the moment, but I knew that eventually I would need to talk to him about what had happened and about what had happened to Paige that he knew and wasn't telling me. Clearly, he knew more than I did, but he wasn't letting on. Why, I couldn't say. Perhaps he was afraid of hurting me, or perhaps it was such catastrophic news that he thought it would obstruct his investigation. Maybe he just couldn't face it for its consequences. Whatever the case, I knew I would eventually need that knowledge. For the moment, though, I could be content asking about the aftereffects of whatever had happened.

"I guess this might sound like a silly question, Luke, but how did you go from that little kid to who you are now?" He looked at me and smiled, laughing.

"I really don't think I'm too different. Well, maybe I am, I don't know. I don't think about that too often. I knew that I had to work at things. I wanted to be stronger, and I guess

I always felt like what had happened back in childhood was my personal failing, and because of that, I fear that I became somewhat obsessed. It was always about getting better at something. I guess I just had something to prove." I felt what he was saying and identified with it deeply in my soul. Though I had previously suspected we were birds of a feather, I didn't know how deeply it ran. For all intents and purposes, we were in exactly the same place as one another. Just two people broken by circumstance. I thought it was astonishing that we could speak like this to one another, considering the damage we had undoubtedly received to our souls.

We both sat like that in silence for a few minutes. Eventually, he turned his face toward mine as the sun slowly crawled over the trees. "I promised you we'd head out and get you clothes today. What do you say? You want to go to town?" He had caught me just when I was taking a sip of coffee, so I eagerly nodded my head, but I couldn't stop wondering, what was he keeping from me?

25

For my entire life, I was essentially constrained to two towns: Gainesville and Bayfield.

I didn't know the name of this little town, but I found it irresistibly charming. There were no large buildings, and everything had the distinct mark of the local soul. It's not as though the places I lived in were massive cities or anything like that. Still, they were subject to the kind of expansion and transformation one would expect over the years, sometimes not for the better, affecting a community's history and changing its neighborhood characteristics. In any suburb or township here, though, it seemed to almost skip over the idyllic small markets, mom-and-pop stores, and restaurants. There was a profound sense of community that I could pick up on just by walking the streets.

Clothes shopping was interesting because I had never really gone shopping for clothes for any reason except practical ones. I was always looking for things that could adequately conceal my handgun or something that would look professional. I was pragmatic by nature, but now, I had other thoughts. I really wanted to see how I could look for Luke, and I wanted to look my best. By the end of the day and four hours later, I had gotten several new outfits. It was by far the longest excursion for clothing I had ever made in my life since my childhood.

Back then, I loved playing dress-up and putting on makeup, but all that died when I lost Paige. I had never grieved for that loss before, but now I was coming back into contact with a part of myself that had almost felt dead. It was as though I could stretch out and say hello to it, and I loved that. A large part of me wanted to thank Luke from the bottom of my heart for bringing me back to a place of humanity that I didn't know I could reach again.

However, part of me thought Luke was probably dealing with the same dilemma. He wasn't well-adjusted either, and I could tell by his actions that he was still very awkward. He didn't know how to process his emotions for me the same way I didn't know how to process mine for him, and at least that put us on the same playing field. So many times that day, I came out of a changing room to ask him what he thought of my outfit, only to find him beat red in the face, unable to say anything but, "Yep, it looks good!" That would have been a disappointing reply from someone else or maybe in another circumstance, but seeing how he looked at me and how awkward he was, it was endearing, and I found it endlessly cute.

We decided to stop at a small ice cream parlor and pick up the ingredients for lunch when we returned. As soon as we arrived back at the cabin, I decided that it would be nice for me to change and really wear these new clothes to full effect. By the time I had gone through that, he had already whipped up an amazing restaurant-worthy lunch. Luke hadn't been lying when he said he could cook; in fact, he could cook fantastically.

According to him, his dad wasn't much of a cook, and his mom was always so busy with work that he had to learn to support the house. As we sat eating, I thought to myself dreamily, what if this is what life could be? What if, when all of this was said and done, we could retire to a comfortable existence with long, lazy days like this where we could just enjoy each other's company?

My feelings for him ran deep, and I wanted to find a way to act on them, but I didn't know how to as I had no experience in the matter, so when he was doing dishes, I walked up behind him and clumsily wrapped my arms around his chest. He stammered a bit and turned back toward me. "Olivia, are you okay?" He was clearly flustered, and that was okay. I was too.

I had no smooth way of saying what I wanted or articulating my feelings, and I fear that it ended up coming out in one of the clumsiest ways it could have, but that also was okay. "Luke, I'd like to spend the night in your room."

"It's not even dark out yet, Olivia."

I nodded my head. "I know."

I could feel him swallowing, as I wanted him to clarify his feelings, feelings he'd hardly know how to say. He stared so intensely into my eyes, almost as if he wanted to memorize how I looked before his lips touched mine. He smelled of spice and a musky, masculine scent that was uniquely his. The world around us went silent, long enough for us to hear our beating hearts, mine, then his, our bodies so close while barely touching each other. I felt so much in that moment, so close, he needed only to whisper, "Can I kiss you?" His whisper reverberated throughout my entire body, awakening parts of me I never knew existed, as our lips met with a passion so instantaneous and urgent. It held a power in itself, forcing me back against the kitchen wall, where I helplessly surrendered with my eyes clenched shut as he took me in his arms and carried me feverishly upstairs to his bedroom. "I love you, Olivia. I've always loved you."

26

I wished these days would not end, but deep down, I knew it was only a small piece of calm before the storm.

As much as I yearned for those days to continue, it wasn't possible. The more time I spent at the lake with Luke, the more my recollection became perfect. I was becoming fully aware of the abnormal nature of Zeus; more importantly, the only places that weren't clear were those I most desperately wanted answers for. Still, even at this point, I couldn't recall what had happened to Paige, or Luke, for that matter. All I wanted was to know what had happened, and my end goal was still to find Paige.

I would be lying if I said that I wasn't becoming frustrated. I was quietly becoming livid, not only because of my inability to uncover the truth, but because surely Luke knew something. Yet every time I questioned him, he became evasive. It was easy to tell that he was hiding something from me, which hurt. While at that cabin, I had bared my soul to him, and he had almost entirely done the same . . . almost. Whenever I brought up Paige, Luke became pensive and withdrawn, as though something was begging to escape from his mouth. He never outright denied knowledge, instead deflecting, telling me I needed to find my own answers. "I'm sure that if you can remember what happened by your own power, everything will fall into place. I'm convinced that your mind holds the key to taking down this cult."

In some sense, I was flattered that he had so much faith in me. For a while, that flattery, mixed with my already existing love for him, kept my frustration from bubbling over, but as the days passed into weeks and my other memories took on greater definition, I couldn't hold back my feelings. Perhaps it was because what I remembered was so cryptic and strange, and the traumatic memories taunted me so intensely. Most of the memories I had uncovered leading up to whatever had happened stuck out because of their distinct paranormal quality. I had already accepted that my imaginary friend was not truly imaginary. Still, I was shocked at how much blatant strangeness I could accept once framed properly.

After that initial exposure and my mother's explanation, I told her when I saw "the man" or "the unicorn," until eventually, to me, he became Zeus. My mother was such a lovely woman, and she didn't ever make me feel strange; instead, she joined me in my play, though she never could have known what I was truly experiencing. She began to teach me nursery rhymes and songs that would calm me and keep me safe when I was scared. Looking back, I began to sing these songs when I wanted to see Zeus. I suppose, in some odd way, I had made my own rules to summon the creature.

In a child's mind, it was simply a song that would attract a friend, but looking back through the eyes of adulthood, it was as though I had created a ritual to bring him close to me. I hadn't thought of those lullabies for years and years, and now all I could think of when I remembered them was if they would still work. Did the creature still remember me, and would it remember those melodies? Pondering the thought was exciting, but that part of me came only from a sense of childhood innocence. It only took moments for it to be replaced with a cold dread of the reality of what Zeus was and what he would be like if I saw him again.

The overwhelming issue with recovering these outlandish memories is that even though I was sure that these events happened in my past, it was very difficult to look at them as though they happened to me. Instead, I found myself forced into the role of a passive observer, as though I was looking at a movie or some other detached media. Simply put, it didn't feel real to me yet, so the idea of having this so close to me, potentially so easily accessible, was blatantly terrifying. I instinctively felt as though I was always standing at a crossroads between reality and a dream and that all I needed to do was utter the right words to break down this fabricated sense of separation. However, I was always too scared to act upon the impulse, fearing for what remained of my sanity.

No matter how strange or outlandish these memories were, it didn't help. I still could not fill in what had happened, and because of that, I couldn't find any sense of peace. It was only a matter of time until the tension I felt was ready to explode. I hadn't kept track of how long it had been since I came to the cabin. I knew that it had at least been four weeks. When morning dawned on that particular day, I had been haunted by nightmares of complacency and felt anxious and antsy. All I wanted was to get to the bottom of what I could not remember. Of course, this had become an almost daily affair. Luke's patience in the situation was impressive, but it was inevitable that things would eventually come to a heated confrontation.

I asked the same question I had asked countless times before. "Please just tell me what happened. Where is Paige? Do you know? Can you give me any clue?" I was feeling particularly desperate. I needed him to give me something. Instead, he just looked at me sadly, shaking his head.

"Olivia, if I could give you any information, I would, but I cannot. You must remember this on your own. As long as your memories are incomplete, we are fighting against unknowns. You're the only person who should know where to find these bastards. You still don't know where they took you before coming to Bayfield?" Perhaps it was the way he dismissed me, or maybe it was his authoritative tone. I didn't know where they had taken me all those years ago. I still didn't remember it, and I was hoping that when this information was back in place, I would have that knowledge, but regardless, that's not what I was worried about. I wanted to fulfill what I said I would. I wanted to find Paige Phillips. Whatever the case was, how he handled it this time made me completely enraged.

Before I knew it, I was yelling. "No, Luke, I don't remember! Maybe I would if you helped me just a little bit! Things are supposed to be a give and take in this sort of relationship, but all I'm doing is giving, and every time I ask for help, you won't give it to me!" I immediately regretted what I was saying because I knew it wasn't true. I could also see that my words were hitting deeply and that Luke was hurt, but even if I knew I was wrong and I was being cruel, that didn't help alleviate the anger.

I bit my lower lip, turning away from Luke's face. Ever since things had become more serious between us, he had become softer and taken on the role of a deeply affectionate and loving partner. As he had let down his internal barriers, though, it seemed that my words were more and more effective at hurting him. I knew I was abusing the trust built between us, but I was frustrated and had no other recourse. Time was not helping to heal the wound in my mind. There was some blockage greater than any I had previously overcome that kept any memories of what had happened to me a secret. I couldn't help but wonder if this was the true secret of the conditioning the cult had given me—if any truly dangerous knowledge that could lead to incrimination was scrubbed so thoroughly from my memory that there would be no hope of bringing it back.

I knew that I needed space to clear my mind but also a plan. If I could just get the space now, I thought, then I could maintain a calm composure and come back to tell Luke about my worries, and then we could start to strategize together. Before any of that, though, I knew I needed to sort out the anger that was now beginning to surface. I lacked any of the strengths of interpersonal relationships that would typically come from having a large friend group or intimacy with people around me. As such, I carried anger in a way that did not make it easy to be around others. I was, to put it simply, terrible at compartmentalizing. I was slowly working on this, and gradually, it was getting better as I opened up more to the person I loved, but it was no simple task.

I thought hard about how to handle the situation I now found myself in. How could I make things right? I couldn't do it quickly; that was the truth, but I had to find some way to put a temporary Band-Aid on what I had said as I tried to collect myself. Given my current mental state, I sighed and turned back toward Luke, trying to conjure up the sweetest smile I could. "Look, I'm sorry. I'm not trying to snap at you; I'm just nearing my wit's end with all of this. I think I need a bit of time on my own. I'm going to go to town and get some supplies." It was a beautiful day out, and a walk or just getting out, in general, would probably help bring me back to a more normal state of calm. To his credit, Luke remained calm despite the obvious distress I'd caused him, and certainly, he didn't look angry. He nodded and tossed me the keys to his car.

"Sorry that I can't be of more help to you, Olivia. Please do what you need to."

I nodded and turned my heel, walking out the door. Inside, I was wondering how I could make it up to him and feel grateful despite the anger, but I also knew that right now wasn't the time to try to fix things.

As I had thought, the outside air was fresh and sweet, and the wind carried a sense of nostalgia that brought me back to a calmer place. I hadn't gotten entirely used to driving Luke's car, but it wasn't bad. If anything, it was much more responsive than the old sedan I was used to. I tried to focus on my surroundings as I drove down the gravel road that eventually would lead into town. Sights, sounds, and smells helped anchor me to the present and served as pleasant reminders of a world that existed outside the chaos of my head. I rolled the windows down, and the smell that drifted off the breeze told me that rain was coming. Perhaps, I thought, the rain would come down and wash away my current irritable mood, replacing it with a new and bright outlook. It was silly and naive to think, but at times, I liked taking hope and comfort in the naivete that I could still produce.

The town was particularly quiet. I still hadn't learned its name, even after all the time here. I could only think it was because I didn't want to know where "here" was. There's certainly something to be said for the comfort that comes with the element of escape. When one's surroundings are simply pleasant without being associated with an earthly location, it allows one to relax fully. No comparison to everyday life needs to be made because you are in someplace other than the normalcy of your surroundings and routine.

Luke had shown me sometime before that a small local grocery store on the main stretch of road made up the town square. *Grocery* perhaps was the wrong term, though, as I thought of it more as a general store. Whatever its actual identity, Eden's Organics was a charming place to stop. It had the heart and soul of a small-town community that couldn't be forced or formulated. It wasn't so much outdated or a throwback as it simply had a different atmosphere from what you would find in the suburbs or the city. After spending so much time in Florida, the local eccentricities of other places in the country were endearing, especially for someone like me, who had no knowledge or interest in traveling until this whole fiasco had begun.

Yes, it's true. I liked the little town quite a bit and the little store. It always put me in a good mood to wander the small aisles and look at locally grown and produced goods. It was strange that I felt a sudden chill run up me as I walked into the small building and was met with the distinct impression that I needed to leave. To a certain degree, I was used to these premonitions, as they were mostly phantom pangs from my troubled past, but in this case, they had all of the red flags of a true gut instinct that was screaming to me from reality.

Cautiously, I looked around me, surveying the locals and trying to find anything that did not fit in, something that reeked of a spiritual divergence, which I was accustomed to feeling. Where I crossed with my eyes, however, spoke nothing to the depraved hidden world of cults and murder that haunted me, so I was left standing there, on guard against something I could not see. It was as though someone was staring at me menacingly, just outside of my line of vision. Worse still, I could feel the presence growing brutally closer as the seconds ticked by.

As though I was physically struck, the sense of danger peaked, and I, against my will, turned back toward the entrance. Standing in the doorway to the building was a tall, silhouetted figure, utterly dark and featureless against the white light that was cast from the sky. Though I could not process what was happening yet, I was extremely terrified, and though I wished to scream, I could not muster any sound. The figure stepped through the threshold into the building's entrance.

Outside, it began to rain.

27

I would have thought by this point in my life, after seeing so much that the average person would deem impossible, or at the very least disturbing, I would be hardened against anything that would come to me, but that was not the case.

The human mind does not work that way. It is never completely safe from a shock. It only weakens, building up superficial walls around itself, trying to act as a cushion in the case of the next terror. However, when that next true horror comes to visit the mind, it has no real defense and has been weakened as a whole. I think this is what causes the mind to erode over time. In line with my theory, I was reacting to this far worse than I had previously, although there were other factors.

Luke and I had driven an entire day. We had told no one of our movements. No one should have known where we were. There was no possible way to track us, yet this figure stood before me, a grim apparition of impossibility and wrongness. It was not simply the deformity of the man who stood before me that made me afraid, nor the sense of déjà vu.

It was not even the fact that no one else around me seemed to notice how disfigured and terrifying the creature standing in front of the exit was, but it was the fact that I had seen this man before. When I had last seen him, he had been shot, and I had fled, terrified but certain of his death. The mocking smile that this hideous thing now wore said everything I needed to know because, without any words, he was mocking me, saying, "You're an idiot to think I was dead." I couldn't manage anything, not even a whimper.

I was trying to brace myself for what would come next, expecting an attack or perhaps an attempted abduction, but that did not come. Instead, the thing walked over to me and placed a hand delicately on my shoulder, lowering itself to my level to meet me, eye to eye. This did nothing to make me more comfortable, for his appearance was terrifying, and his eyes were like staring into pools of tar that somehow reflected starlight. "Olivia, there's something I'd like to talk to you about out front if you don't mind." There was no glee or joviality in the voice but also no sneer I had heard before. Numbly, I nodded and found myself following Todd Decker outside.

Perhaps even more shocking than the initial appearance of the looming presence was his attitude as I followed him out into the rain. Though I had no way to defend myself, I was still preparing for an attack. I didn't know how to react when, as if he was simply an ordinary man, he looked up to the sky, clicked his teeth, and lifted a hand out of his trench coat pocket, staring at me in disappointment. "The forecast didn't say anything about rain today. I'm sorry, this isn't exactly the best day for a walk, now, is it? It could be worse though. I mean, under the overhang, we won't get too wet talking. Do you mind if I smoke?" Of anything I could expect or attempt to prepare for, how was I supposed to deal with this inhuman monstrosity talking to me as if it was an average day at the office? I was stupefied and had no idea how to react.

"Uh . . . sure, I don't mind." Truthfully, I didn't even know why I was talking, but something told me that when someone asked a question, it was only common courtesy to answer, and right now, my body and mind were acting off of those basic social instincts. At my approval, Decker nodded, taking a pack of cigarettes from his other trench coat pocket and lighting it before leaning back against the building. "You smoke?" The grotesque, deformed figure shrugged its shoulders before looking at me. I don't know how long I stood there, but I became distinctly aware of the weight of my feet holding my body in position, feeling myself drifting into a deluded consciousness. I had no words.

"I never really tried to kick the habit. It's not like it's really hurting me. What's the worst that will happen? You think I'm going to get cancer and die?" He smiled in that horrible, distorted way he did on the trail. I looked away. It didn't matter how casual he was, Decker was a monster and exuded an air of danger and palpable wrongness. I felt complete and utter distaste standing next to him. It was not simply a matter of personal preference or trauma, but rather an instinctual repugnance comparable to what one would feel next to a rotting body.

As far as I was concerned, whatever Decker had become, he was a tumor on reality. I worked hard to suppress my revulsion and stand my ground. As I brought myself to look at his distorted face, our eyes locked, and I felt a new wave of goosebumps. He took a long drag on his cigarette. "Wow, aren't you going to ask me something? I know you have questions you want answers to, right?"

My eyes widened as I blurted out, "Wait, you're here to answer my questions?"

He shrugged, looking away from me and into the rain, steadily getting heavier. "Not as such, but I have an offer to make." I felt disgusted in the pit of my stomach. I would refuse any offer that this thing would have to make, but still, curiosity burned in my head. I wanted answers. I needed answers at this point, and nothing I was doing was bringing me any closer. Apparently, he took my silence as an indicator to continue. "I'm only here as a favor to Simon." My stomach dropped at the mention of my so-called father's name. "He's worried about you, Olivia, and he thinks the only way he can get you to come home is if he tells it to you straight, a heart-to-heart, father-to-daughter. He said that he's willing to answer any questions you might have. The only catch is that he wants you to come home to talk."

I was terrified at the thought, but at the same time, I was surprised to find myself considering it. Simon Monroe had acted the part of my father for years, and despite the fact that I had found him off-putting at times, he never was overtly dangerous or violent toward me. Still, I didn't know what he was exactly capable of, and I was well aware now that I had never truly known the man who had raised me. Obviously, though, it was a trap; that much was clear. Before I could open my mouth to say no, Decker was already interjecting.

"Are you honestly making so much progress with that Hayes boy that you no longer want answers? Things must be going fantastically on regaining your memory then." I knew he was mocking me, and I knew he was trying to take stabs at me to get me angry, but it was working nonetheless. Suddenly, the gaunt creature barked an awed voice, and I realized he was chuckling. "If you knew what hand Luke played in all this, then I don't think you'd be looking at him so favorably." My heart sank. There's no way Luke was involved in this. He had protected me, time after time.

"Shut up, freak! I trust Luke, and he trusts me! You don't know anything about him!" Decker stomped the butt of the cigarette he had just finished smoking, taking another one out and lighting it. His face, though difficult to read for its lack of normal human features, was a mixture of amusement and annoyance.

"Hmm. Maybe old Todd doesn't understand. In that case, I'm sure that old Luke has told you all about what happened on that fateful day. He's told you where Page is and what condition she's in, right? Or maybe I was right at first, and you don't know him as well as you think you do."

"I . . . Well, he . . ." It was true that Luke wouldn't say anything about what had happened. In every way I could try to rationalize why that was, it didn't change the fact that he hadn't told me the entirety of the truth when I had told him everything. The monster shook his head in what seemed like fabricated pity.

"It's so sad watching you be manipulated like this. I want you to really think about something, Olivia. What have we actually done to you?" The question came from nowhere, and I felt rage welling up in my chest, but before I could speak, he stopped me, holding a hand in front of him. "Let me finish. We look scary, I know, and, yes, we did take you from your home, but many children are taken from their homes when they're small. We saw that you had potential and wanted to see that you were raised right. It might seem like you've been protected by that boy every time you've encountered us; after all, we're scary beings, right? But the truth of the matter is different! You just assumed that if we were going to find you, we'd hurt you. In reality, every time we've tried to talk to you, that boyfriend of yours has decided to shoot someone!"

This couldn't be right. I found myself reviewing what happened again and again in my head, going over the events. No, I was attacked! There was reason for him to do what he had done. These people were evil. They were monsters! "You're going to sit here and try to tell me that this has all been some kind of misunderstanding when Rebecca tried to kill me?"

Decker shook his head, turning to me and throwing down the cigarette with a look of displeasure. "You're lumping us all together, Olivia. Who do you think Rebecca worked for, us? No, we knew about her and we did things with her, but she wasn't one of ours. No, no, she worked with agent Luke Hayes. That man will do anything to manipulate his marks. He's playing you like a fiddle."

Again, I felt the world around me threatening to cave in on itself. I didn't believe what this monster was saying, not by a long shot, but still, he had planted a very real seed of doubt that was doing its job inside my heart. I was in love with Luke, and deep down, I knew that he was an ally, but at the same time, I also knew that he was keeping something from me. He continually insisted that I needed to make this breakthrough on my own, so in a way, he had pushed me to this decision. I would have to be on my own, just like I was before he showed up. I realized I had been too complacent and relied too heavily on him—this was my investigation. I looked up into the beast's face, seeing the seeming delight in those strange, beady eyes. "You're full of shit, Decker. It is true, though, that I have questions that Simon could answer."

Again, that predatory smile bloomed across the once-human creature's face. "Well, I suppose the details don't matter much as long as you accept my proposal." He reached into his breast pocket, placing the cigarettes inside and taking out a slip of torn paper. "All you need to do is go to this address. Don't worry, I'll make the necessary arrangements to ensure a nice meeting." With that, the gangly being turned on his heel and began to walk away.

"Wait, I have one question for you." Almost mechanically, this monstrosity of a man stopped in mid-stride, turning back around on his heel and facing me.

"Make it quick. I have places to be and things to do." Any fear I felt from this hideous thing quickly turned to outrage. Where did any of these people get off acting like they did? He had said he spent all of this time coming to find me, and once he did, he walked away and acted like I was an annoyance. Again, I had to fight the instinctual revulsion from dealing with him.

"Why doesn't anyone seem to notice your kind, whatever that is? We're in broad daylight, and you look awful. There's no way you can go under the radar like that!"

Decker smiled again, but it wasn't the mocking, semi-jovial expression this time. Instead, there was an element of pride, a maliciousness that was less based on a sense of cruelty and more on the fact that he knew something important I did not. It was the look of someone who had achieved something great, at least in their own eyes. "That's just a silly question. Did anyone notice Zeus when you played with him?"

My heart skipped a beat. What was he implying? Was he trying to say that he was the same? Before I could fully process what he said and articulate with a follow-up question, he simply vanished into thin air. For a long moment, I stood there on the sidewalk, considering whether I had gone insane, whether I had been speaking to my own delusional hallucination. Looking next to me, though, I saw the crushed cigarette butts left behind. No, there was something far more sinister afoot. I sighed. Great, another thing that I had to get to the bottom of, but it was all going to be over soon. I hoped that if I could see Simon, the man I had only known as my "father," then I would finally get answers.

28

I left right away using Luke's car. I knew that I couldn't keep what I would do a secret from him if I went back to the cabin, but also, at this point, I didn't know whether or not I could fully trust him with the information I'd received. If everything went well, I'd return with his car in a couple of days. A part of me hurt deeply. I knew this would be better with him by my side, but I also knew how dangerous the situation I was going into was, and I would be lying if I didn't point out that the words of that creature had swayed my thoughts about Luke. Certainly not that I believed Decker, but I also knew that Luke was keeping things from me, and if I were truly to give him all my trust, I would need answers to my questions first.

Trying to find my bearings, I aimlessly stumbled upon the ramp to the interstate. The drive back down to Florida felt far more grueling than it had been coming up. Perhaps it was because I had some idea of what was coming, of what I'd have to deal with, or maybe it was just that I was the one behind the wheel this time. Whatever the case was, by the time I had finally crossed into Florida, I was stiff and anxious. My handgun was on my hip like it always was, but it didn't give me any of the comforts it used to. Now I knew there were things in this world that even bullets couldn't deter.

The address I had been given led to an abandoned industrial park located approximately five miles away from the Bayfield Police Department. It was a place I had passed many times while on patrol or going to and from different parts of the city but had never paid any attention to. I had noticed the pattern with this cult. They always seemed to use neglected structures, these places that drew no one but these despicable people. It was chilling to me that someplace so close to home was actually a staging point for something so heinous.

As I exited the car, the reality of the situation I was stumbling into started to dawn on me fully. As I took those unsure steps toward the entrance of the dilapidated building that once served as a dispatch hub, I was uncontrollably shaking and shivering, though I hoped it was subtle enough that no one watching could tell.

The door to the building was open, and close inspection revealed that it was marked with the same symbolic type symbol of a bird that I had found inside both the file and the journal. In the absence of anyone else there, I decided that I was probably expected and free to walk in. It was no sooner than I had thought this and stepped to the door that two robed men, their faces obscured by masks, stepped in at my sides. I expected them to grab me, but then I realized they were just bowing slightly. "Welcome, Miss Monroe."

Internally, I felt a pang of disgust and anger. "It's Miss Harper." Of course, the men didn't respond, but they may have gotten the message. Even if they didn't, then surely Simon would when he saw me. The two figures led me down a long corridor to an uncovered set of stairs. The stairway went on for some time, looping in on itself, continuing in a zigzag formation much like the stairwells of fire exits, except this one continued going down further into the earth. Eventually, these stairs ended in an ornate carved wooden door. From the looks of it, I assumed it was either made of oak or mahogany. Whatever it was, it was extremely flamboyant and certainly expensive. Again, I felt a sense of revulsion. There was something inherently decadent about the way the cult went about things that made my skin crawl. A part of me was reminded of how conspiracy theorists talked about shadowy organizations like the Illuminati, who are thought to be linked to pulling the strings of government. However, this was real and far more terrible.

No one had to open the door as it began to swing open. Behind it were several other larger figures who I immediately recognized due to their strange, searing eyes. Even in their heavy ceremonial robes, masks, and hoods, it was obvious that these were the same kinds of creatures I'd seen back at the abandoned house and that Todd Decker had become. Ten of them stood in the doorway, and that sheer number in one place was enough to make my blood run cold. I had no clue what made them the way they were, though it was without a shadow of a doubt that it was something that violated the very laws of nature.

As they cleared to the sides of the aisle, which I now could see was furnished with a red carpet of extraordinary quality, I noted the great reverence they moved with. It was as though they had practiced the movements very precisely and were now acting them out ceremonially. It wasn't all surprising, considering that they were a religious order. Still, though, it sent chills down my spine. Only one of the more prominent figures remained, standing in the middle of the vaulted doorway. This one's robes were slightly more ornate, and he stood just slightly taller than the others. Something about his demeanor and disposition immediately struck me as familiar. And I realized that this was Decker in more formal attire. "The meeting place has been prepared. Follow me, initiate."

I had no clue what he was talking about, but it seemed like the smartest move at that moment was to play along. Every time I had heard him speak before, his voice was garbled. Now, however, it rang clear, still inhuman and grotesque, but there was more strength to it. I walked forward as he led the way, feeling myself surrounded on both sides by one of the more normally sized robed men. Now inside this hidden elaborate vault, I could see it was not a repurposed space at all but had been made with great care to be a lodge of sorts.

The ceiling was covered in fantastical and grotesque murals that seemed to dance before my eyes. The walls were covered in art pieces depicting bodies rising from the dead and monstrous deformities dancing through rings of fire. Other pieces depicted the mythical golden bird I had seen on the symbols, conjuring visions of rebirth, rising from the ashes of its old self. I could only think I was witnessing some sort of bizarre resurrection or a life-and-death transformation ritual.

Eventually, the long corridor terminated in a vast room. It was like an amphitheater, appearing as a domed structure with columns holding the ceiling at its edges. The chamber was primarily lit by dangling chandeliers of beautiful design. The room's layout reminded me of a Senate, or perhaps a courthouse, where a large, elevated bench with many seats inside gave way to a more general seating area with an open floor before them. In this case, though, it seemed the room's layout had been somewhat changed, with a heavy, rounded table placed in the middle of what would have been a standing area. The table was surrounded by high, extremely fine leather chairs, and sitting in each one was a figure, some of which I recognized and others I did not.

My heart sank as I looked from face to face, realizing just how deep the conspiracy truly went. On the far side of the table were Cooper Harrison and Conrad Hudson. Between the two of them was another seat directly opposed to the one prepared for me. In this chair sat Simon Monroe. He looked like I had never seen him before. Gone was the anxiety and gruffness I expected from him, replaced by a joviality that felt wrong given all my memories of the man. I looked at him baffled because usually, I knew the man to bury himself in his hands, to be on the edge of weeping, to be hindered by a sense of worry about life in general. And here he was, wrapped in an air of confidence, talking to Cooper and Conrad like old friends, although I suppose they were.

It took Simon a moment to look up; however, it was only because of Decker clearing his throat with a truly awful sound. When he noticed me, though, he stood up and made a gesture of welcome, extending his arms to the side as if he would hug me, though the meeting table separated us. "Olivia, I'm so happy that you've decided to come. Oh, how I've worried about you. Please sit down. I'm sure that we have a lot to discuss." I didn't like this at all. To put it plainly, everything about my father's persona that he was wearing now seemed superficial and yet more genuine than what I had seen of him. It was as though underneath the veneer of a man tortured by life around him, there was actually a callous, calculating man who cared almost nothing for what happened around him. A self-serving sociopath, that was the impression that I got.

I sat down without returning his greeting. I needed to collect my thoughts and prioritize what I would say despite what I may have felt inside. I knew that letting myself run wild could only lead to bad results. I took a deep breath, knowing what I needed to ask and what was most important. I was also attempting to get a good idea of my actual situation here, potential escape routes, how I could fight if things were to turn wrong. Bleakly, I realized I had almost no recourse. I swallowed as my eyes darted around the room, feeling a lump in my throat. I regretted coming here and couldn't help but think I had made an awful mistake.

Simon took out a small rod that looked like something between a gavel and a symbol of a king's authority and struck the table several times, bringing attention to himself and silencing the rest of the robed men and women. "My dear friends, I believe it's time to call this meeting into session. As you all know, this is not a normal meeting, and I am sorry for the short notice, but my daughter, Olivia, has questions about our order, and I thought it was only right that we answer them." He gestured toward me. I felt sick. I hated the way he was treating me and this entire situation. He was making light of everything I had gone through by simply treating this like any other day.

To him, it was clear that my pain and suffering meant nothing, that this was just part of the process . . . and he still had the audacity to call me his daughter. If I didn't have a high level of control of my emotions at that moment, I think I would have pulled out my gun and shot him right there, but I bit my tongue and balled my fists, trying to keep a level head. I realized that everyone around the table was looking at me. Looking over my shoulder, I saw that Decker was standing by my side, almost how you would expect an aide or butler to stand near their master. It was, to say the least, surreal, and in a moment of absurdity, I was suddenly aware that I seemed quite underdressed for this setting. I frantically stamped the thought out as soon as it had come into my mind, standing so I could take the floor. Simon interjected as I stood. "Good, getting right into it, we'll do the question-and-answer session before the initiation."

"What initiation?" That wasn't supposed to be my first question, but I was taken aback enough that it overrode what I was going to say beforehand. The robed figures all looked at one another, chuckling. It was as though I was a young child who had stumbled into a meeting in a business place and asked a silly question. I didn't care for their attitude. It didn't matter. What mattered was that I got answers, no matter how condescending their delivery was.

Conrad Hudson stood up to answer my question, the very man who had mentored me for the past several years and who had taken an oath of office that included serving society and safeguarding lives. This man I now saw before me was not the chief I knew from past family get-togethers, but a dangerous stranger involved in these brutal cult killings and child abductions, now reduced to nothing more than a murderer. I still didn't know how to process seeing him here. "He's referring to your initiation, Olivia. We wouldn't have offered this meeting if we didn't intend to bring you fully into the fold. We're here to recognize your efforts." It was only a partial answer, but their ulterior motive became quite clear. They had set up this meeting to reclaim me. That was painfully obvious.

29

"What exactly are the Disciples of the Rising Phoenix? Why did you take me from my home?" I decided that I would keep the questions coming at a brisk pace. I wanted to learn all I could without getting sucked into the atmosphere they were trying to cultivate. I wasn't here for their mind games. I was here for answers.

Simon reclined into his chair and answered with a contented look, "The Disciples of the Rising Phoenix is, for all intents and purposes, a social and religious organization that seeks to find people who are gifted in seeing things that are not ordinary. We seek out people who can see extra-dimensional entities because we have found good evidence that these entities are the key to unlocking full human potential and even immortality." I thought my mouth was going to drop to the floor. That was perhaps the most far-fetched explanation I could have ever imagined. It explained why I was a target, and Paige, for that matter. If they were trying to find people who could bridge this gap between the seen and the unseen, they must have believed that it could lead to enlightenment or even the reversal of death. And that would give them the necessary motivation to commit such inhuman atrocities.

"All of this happened because I could see Zeus?" Again, I felt the regret, the pangs of guilt that came from knowing so much had happened because I simply couldn't stay quiet. All I wanted was to see Paige, to apologize to her.

This time, Cooper chimed in with an answer, putting up his hand in the matter-of-fact way he always did. "Well, no, it's not just because you could see your friend; it's because you could interact with him and coax him into doing things for you that affected the world around us. Simply seeing something isn't enough for us. Plenty of people report seeing outlandish things. They could be making it up. It could be a figment of their imagination. They could just be children. That's not going to decide whether someone has extra sensory perception. Only when we figured out that what you were seeing was the genuine article did we take an active interest in you."

He said this all cheerily, as though it was an explanation given to someone eager and happy. The lack of awareness that any of them showed was stunning, almost as much as it was revolting. I went over what he said in my mind. I was starting to get a fuller picture of what must have happened, but there were still blanks. I needed to find the right questions to answer those pieces.

I gestured to the monstrosity standing behind my chair. "What exactly happened to Decker and all of the others like him? What are they?" I knew enough to realize that they weren't human. These weren't just costumes, and they didn't just have differences in their anatomy. They were truly eccentric in how they interacted with the world around them. Aside from that, everything I could tell showed that they were almost invisible to those who didn't have this second sight they talked about.

Surprisingly, this question resulted in hushed conversation and murmuring around the table. I wondered if what I had brought up was the topic of some debate. Eventually, though, the hammer was struck a couple more times, and silence fell across the meeting again. Like a scholar pondering a particularly complex subject, Simon Monroe was thoughtfully rubbing his chin. "Well, Olivia, we refer to them as *inner disciples*. Our interest in these entities is not just in trying to make contact with them or studying them. If you don't have the aptitude to do so, you simply can't. Our studies and powers are dedicated to and derived from the reclamation of old wisdom, traditions that tell us how to leave our normal state of humanity behind."

Suddenly, my mind returned to that old, dilapidated, abandoned hell house. The blood stains on the doors and the symbols written in gore. The ritual murders that had been suddenly cropping up in the tri-state area. "So, to do that, you commit murder for blood rituals?"

Conrad chuckled. "You are a good detective, Olivia, although you're being a bit dramatic. In most cases, our participants are fully willing. They know the risks coming in, and they also know the benefits if things go correctly. A body that doesn't age, even if it isn't very aesthetically pleasing, and the ability to regenerate most wounds is a tantalizing reward to most." All of the robed faces nodded shrewdly in agreement.

I was starting to have serious trouble not letting my anger get the better of me, but still, I kept myself in check. "If it's such an honor, why do you all look normal?"

Again, it was Simon who answered. "It's not as though every one of us would be ready to sacrifice our apparent humanity just for power. Everything we've seen suggests there are greater depths to this and a more perfect state that one could reach. Aside from that, at least some of our higher-ranking members need to be able to remain active in the world at large. Otherwise, we couldn't compete for our own interests." To me, it sounded like they were cowards, using the members who were expendable for experiments, and those who were more integral to the running of the operation were the ones who likely profited.

I had learned enough about what happened here. I knew what was going on. I thought I knew what these people were, and I now had enough proof that they were the evil I had envisioned. Now, I needed my largest questions answered. "What did you do to Paige Phillips?" As much as I was trying, I could not keep my voice steady as I asked that fateful question. To my shock, the response around the table was strained and immediate. I had been expecting a unanimous reaction of perhaps laughter or condescension, but instead, the faces looked at each other concerned. Strangely, they looked as though they didn't know the answer to what I was asking.

"Olivia, I thought you were looking into what happened to Paige. Haven't you made any progress on that?" It was Conrad Hudson. He sounded disappointed, almost as if a subordinate had returned and didn't have what you thought they would. What did he mean? Of course, I had been looking into Paige, but they were the ones responsible for what happened to her. If anyone knew, it would be them, right?

Simon was tapping his fingers against the table, and for once, he looked as I remembered him, pensive and somewhat anxious. "Olivia. If we knew where Paige Phillips was, we would have brought her back, the same as we've tried to do with you. I'm sorry if you thought you would get answers to that here, but I genuinely have no clue what happened to her. She was under our surveillance, and she suddenly disappeared along with Luke Hayes."

What? No, that couldn't be true. There was no way. I knew that they had left, but I thought that was the cult's fault, and it was, right? They couldn't have just disappeared with no word. What was Luke not telling me? Did that mean he was fully aware of what had happened to Paige, not just on that day, but her fate? I scrambled for answers in my head but knew that I couldn't focus on this. I had to keep moving on, or else I would get bogged down and pulled into their world of insanity. "What about my mother? What did you do to her and my real father?" I knew I was running out of time to ask these questions.

At the mention of my mother, Simon smiled but seemed to ignore the second part of the question about my father. "I don't know what Camila Harper is doing these days, and I don't know if she's okay, but I can certainly say that I didn't do anything to harm her when we took you."

My heart fluttered in my chest for a moment. "Wait, so you lied when you said my mother died?" Simon nodded his head. This was the first piece of great news I had gotten since this investigation started. Aside from the revelation that Paige Phillips might have been alive, for once, this was positive. I felt as though I might cry. I looked down at my wristwatch, trying to hide my emotions. There were perhaps ten or fifteen minutes left until things would get hectic. "What do you all need from me exactly? Why me instead of someone else?"

My adoptive father looked from face to face around the table, nodding, and all of them decided to stand up, looking at me with a great air of importance. "I doubt you've put much thought into this, Olivia, but your gifts are exceptional among the exceptional. Most people might be able to see or interact, but you were able to call one of these entities to you, to bring him to heel. He was not just a plague or something in the corner of your vision. He was not a demon that plagued you during your nightmares. He was a friend that aided you. You have the ability to contact something from beyond the reach of our understanding. What we need from you is that ability. You essentially have what we can only describe as bottled lightning. It is almost impossible for those of us around this table to be able to make any small contact with these creatures. You could bring one of them in the flesh into our midst."

There was an air of electricity and excitement that rose around the table. These monstrous people thought that they were about to fulfill their goal and meet one of these holy, immortal creatures. These people were fools. That was plain and clear to me now as I recalled times with my best friend and our many playdates with the unicorn Zeus. There were a lot of memories that told me more about its nature than I would have ever wanted to know.

I knew now that it was not truly a unicorn, nor was it a man in the lightning. It took on shapes that it thought the people around it would accept. There were times, though, when that veil or illusion slept, times when I remembered looking to where I thought my imaginary friend would be, only to have a nightmare standing in its place. And in those remembrances, I could pinpoint times when the frightening power of this creature was apparent. I may have been friends with the entity known as Zeus when I was a small child, blinded by my own curiosity and innocence, but now, as an adult and someone who understood the ways of the world, I would never willingly wish to make contact with such a creature. The fact that they were inviting such disaster upon themselves and wanting to flirt with the volatile nature of something outside of human understanding was not just idealistic; it was idiotic.

The cold cynicism I felt for those misguided people around me was a shocking new emotion. It was the last place I would expect it, but it sparked a memory. I could suddenly hear a small voice full of strength speaking to me: "Your dad is crazy. I don't know what's happening, but it's not good. I have to get out of here, and I need to help Paige too." Like a pane of glass shattering, suddenly, there was clarity in my mind. I remembered what happened that fateful day.

It was a chaotic memory that wouldn't have even made sense to me if I didn't have the element of the story that I did now. On the day that Paige and Luke had gone away, Luke came to me. He was scraped up and bruised, and he was scared. I had been playing on our favorite trail leading to the lake. He said there were men who knew my father who had gone toward Paige's house. Luckily, he had been nearby along with his dad. The two of them had fought savagely to keep them away from the little girl and her family. He had come to try and find me to take me with them. He said that they needed to go somewhere far away. That's right, Luke's father was also a federal agent, a man with power in high places, but who was honorable, not touched by the corruption of Bayfield. I had agreed to go with them, and I had started down that path to meet them at a rendezvous point. That's when I ran into Todd Decker. What had happened after that,

I still don't know, but I know that they had taken me. I guess they wanted to make sure that day was permanently a jumble in my memories so I would never know what had happened.

I stood in the midst of the fools who made up the cult. They were all talking and laughing with one another. They were so focused on their victory, so pinpointed on the idea that I had silently complied, that they had let down their guard. I paused, knowing that I shouldn't look for revenge, but after all this time, this was going to feel good. I smiled. "Thanks, Dad. You know, this has been a really helpful talk, and I don't think you really know what you're asking for, but I'm going to give it to you." A hush fell across the room, and as I took a deep breath, getting ready to sing, I heard a boom from somewhere upstairs and knew that Luke must have arrived.

30

When dealing with dangerous people, it's always of the utmost importance to ensure that you don't reveal all of your strengths and that you always have something in reserve.

When Todd Decker had come to me in Pennsylvania to try to vie for my favor, asking me to return to Bayfield, it may have hurt my trust in Luke. That was true, but not enough to throw away what I had built with him. I had made the decision to take Luke's car, not his personal vehicle, but his assigned vehicle. I knew from our previous conversations that those cars had trackers on them, and I also knew that given how protective Luke was, when I wasn't back within an hour, he would come out to look for me and then check the vehicle's location.

We had a contingency plan in case I was ever abducted. He would look for my location and bring an entire SWAT team. All this time, down in this subterranean vault, I considered how long it would take for Luke and his friends to come crashing in to ruin their party. Of course, I was worried. There were all of those so-called inner disciples, and they clearly were monsters, but Simon had said they didn't age, not that they were truly immortal. I was betting they had a breaking point; if they did, the heavily armed agents would find it.

Turning around, I wasn't surprised to see that the hulking inner disciples had all left their places around the room, instead going to inspect the disturbance up above. I knew this would be a gamble, the whole thing. There was no guarantee of success or survival. I would have to keep these high-ranking cult members busy, and I knew how I could do it. If I was lucky, I might even take them out, and then, I could look for an opportunity to run back up those stairs. Hopefully, the inner disciples would already be disposed of, and Luke would be leading the charge.

It was hardly a plan, more or less a hopeful assumption, but still, it's what I had to go by. Just as the people around the table started to move from their seats, drawn to the sound from up above, I called out loudly. "Where are you all going? Didn't you want to see what I could bring? I'll tell you right now that you don't need to worry about what's happening outside because I can do exactly what you want me to right here!" A murmur rose amongst the faces, and a feeling of ecstatic revelation and joy filled the room, even as I could hear the distant, piercing gunshots echoing through the ground.

At a gesture from Simon, all of them retook their seats, and the meeting was once again in place. He looked to me for direction. Profound pride on his face. "Please, Olivia. Call him down. Let us see him." He didn't know what he was asking for, but I would happily oblige.

Though I hadn't remembered the words until mere days before, the lullaby moved from my lips naturally. There was an almost hypnotic quality to my voice, and even as chaos fought its way down the stairways and corridors of the cult hideout, a palpable sense of calm descended on the inner chamber. Before my very eyes, as much as anyone else's, I saw that the air above the table began to shift and distort, merging into a silhouette of ethereal quality.

At first, it was in the vague shape of a man before taking a more recognizable form . . . that of a white unicorn. A voice more felt than heard rippled through the room. It was an inhuman but calming voice that I only remembered in the farthest-flung reaches of my childhood memories. "You haven't called on me to play in such a long time, my friend. It's good to see you."

"Thank you, Zeus, but I'm not here to play. These people all wanted to see you. They wanted to see what you really are, but the thing is, they're not friends. They're terrible, terrible people." The cult surrounding me started to stand up, edging closer. They could tell that something was wrong. "Zeus, they've hurt me a lot. They also hurt our other friend Paige and the boy who was always with us. Worse than all of that, they've killed a lot of people."

The shape flickered and shifted, and for a moment, I could see something else behind the form of that unicorn, something that my mind refused to acknowledge. "So you're saying that they're bad people? That they need to go away?" Zeus was always so matter-of-fact and straightforward whenever he talked to me.

It felt like no time had passed, and a wave of childhood innocence washed over me, even though I hadn't seen or heard from him in over twenty years. I smiled and nodded my head. "That's right, Zeus. I'm going to leave. I don't want to see what you look like when you have to deal with these types of degenerates."

The unicorn nodded, and it was no sooner that I had said this than I turned around, and the people around me began to react. From the corners of my eyes, I could see several of them had begun to bleed from their eyes, ears, and nose. Some began to scream and pound on the table, looking at something they could not describe but also could not handle. Others tried running wildly from the room, but something prevented them. I tried to avert my eyes from any of the places where reality seemed to shimmer and shift as they were pulled back toward the center of the table. Behind me, there was a horrifying ear-splitting whistling sound. I knew it was nothing from this world, as I could only think it was a way of summoning a supernatural presence that was making itself known to these cultists.

Whenever Paige and I played as children, Zeus had always come to save us. He was a great lover of children and a great lover of innocence and justice, but that didn't keep him from being a transcendental presence that would deal with what he viewed as evil in a very direct and brutal way. I had given the Disciples of the Rising Phoenix what they wanted. It was their own choice to decide how he would react to them. I ran down the hallway, trying to press out the unreal sounds and sights unfolding behind me, making sure not to catch a glimpse of whatever was hiding behind that disguise. Despite everything that had happened, I found a tear absently falling from my eye. Those people were horrific. They were monsters in their own right, but I don't know if anyone deserved the fate that would befall anything that got too close to a creature like that. Still, though, I couldn't waste time on it. I had to run, so I pushed myself further.

The corridor leading to the staircase was littered with gore. As I began to scale the stairs, I saw several bodies I recognized. Gripped by the overwhelming fear shooting through me, I suddenly thought of the SWAT members, wondering if they were even capable of deterring these creatures. As I continued to climb, I found body after body, hunched and blown apart, that had fallen back down the stairs, and they were unmistakably that of the inner disciples. I crossed one which some explosion had blown apart, probably a grenade or large-caliber round, and absently noted the smile on its face. The strangeness was gone; instead of a monster, it held the shape of an elderly man, twisted and broken.

I averted my eyes, fighting the urge to vomit. The haze of sulfur and gun smoke was sickening and suffocating. I could tell that explosives had been used by the scorch marks littering everything, along with the broken support on the stairs. I was just thankful they carried my weight as I hurried to the top. "Freeze, hands up!" The voice was harsh and coarse, but I recognized it all the same, so throwing my hands up, I called out to it.

"Luke! It's me!" No sooner had I done that than a figure in ballistics armor ran through the haze, grabbing me and pulling me out of the building. Luke tore his helmet off and embraced me, pulling me into a kiss.

"Olivia, oh thank God. What happened?" He was crying as I wiped a tear away.

"I finally came to meet you. Luke, I'm so sorry I couldn't before when we were kids. If I hadn't been abducted by Todd Decker and Simon Monroe, we could have all disappeared together, you, me, and Paige."

The single tear became many, and Luke sobbed heavily, pulling me closer. "You remember!" I realized I was crying, too, and I pulled him in closer. I was finally free. All that remained was to find Paige.

EPILOGUE

I learned from Luke that after that day, he and his father had extricated Paige and her family over to Georgia. Surprisingly, they were about four hours away from Gainesville. Luke had been utterly desperate for me to regain memories of what happened on my own because he knew that if he was going to answer them and I didn't recover them on my own, there would always be a question of whether I could fully trust him. He wanted me to be able to heal instead of just running away.

Years after he left without me, once he had joined the Bureau, Luke tracked down my mother, Camila Harper. Apparently, she was alive and well, and it was from her that he realized I had already been abducted when we first met. After years of going undercover investigating the horrific murders and abductions in the tri-state area, Luke made it his mission to track down this monstrous group of people that called themselves the Disciples of the Rising Phoenix, leading him to the cult's headquarters and one of its leaders, Simon Monroe, the only man I had ever known as my father.

He also found that my biological father, Joel Harper, had been beaten to death a week after my abduction and left for dead in the woods next to my family's home. No one really knew if he was somehow involved with this cult or if it was just an isolated incident, but to this day, Luke still believes that Simon had a hand in the crime, and sadly, my father's death remains a mystery. I vowed that day that, no matter what I had to do or who I had to go through, I would fight to re-open his case and leave no stone unturned to find his killer. He deserved that, and so did my mother.

From what I heard from the recent ambush at the cult's headquarters, it looked as though a particularly gruesome fire burned it, and they weren't able to recover any bodies. With the sheer enormity of this horrific event, I have no doubt the people responsible for tearing apart my childhood are now gone. I thought about all of this from my seat on the plane. It had been about two weeks since the incident, and I had made it clear that I wanted to go and meet my mother. Luke said he wanted time to arrange things so Paige could be there to meet us when we arrived. I was told they all had maintained contact throughout the years, and she had worried about me just as much as I worried about her; however, she had never gone into detective work, instead channeling her empathy and becoming a doctor.

I sat next to Luke and felt a sense of peace for the first time in years. I didn't have a care in my mind except for feeling the eager anticipation of what stood ahead. I went over the details of all that had happened. Everything I had fought for, everything I had endured, how my mind had very nearly gone to the breaking point and back. I also thought of Zeus and wondered what the creature was doing now, although I suppose there was no need to worry. If I knew him, he had probably found another child to help in their play and protect. I don't think I will ever call on him again, and I don't think he will hold it against me either.

As we touched down, I felt my heart pounding in my throat. I knew what was coming but didn't know if I was prepared. Luke looked over at me, seeing the anxiety playing on my face, and hugged me as we got up and retrieved our baggage. He leaned in and kissed me tenderly. "It's a bit late to back out now, Olivia, don't you think? We're finally here."

"I know, but what if I'm not like how they think I'll be? Or what if they're not?" Luke gently placed a finger over my lips. His calm smile told me everything I needed to know, and I knew I had let my emotions get the best of me. Trying to keep calm, I silently told myself . . . "Shake it off, Oliva. It will all be okay. Stop worrying so much."

As we got to the terminal and started heading down the escalator, a face waiting down at the baggage claim immediately stuck out to me. It was a woman about my age, though if you had asked me, I would have assumed she was younger. She had long golden hair and dark eyelashes. Her piercing blue eyes locked with mine, and her angelic face erupted into a smile.

"Livvy!" she cheered boisterously. I was suddenly back in my childhood home, hearing that sweet yet familiar voice calling out from her bedroom window . . . "Livvy, can you come over for a playdate?" I had dreamt of this moment so many times.

Next to her was a woman from the depths of my childhood memories. Though older, tempered by the years, her sweet face was that of a soothing lullaby. She smiled as our eyes met for the first time, her lips trembling through her tear-stained face. As we stepped down from the escalator, the two moved toward us with open arms as I squeezed Luke's hand.

I had finally found what I had been searching for . . . my family . . . my heart . . . my home.

THE END

ACKNOWLEDGMENTS

I want to thank my two children for their unwavering
belief in me, and the writers, teachers, and online
writing communities for their inspiration,
ideas, and encouragement.

I thank my wonderful husband, who said I could,
for the heartfelt support, and all of my family
and friends who said I should.

And, of course, a big thank you to my cherished readers
for keeping me grounded in a place where writing is born,
allowing me to share my passion for storytelling
with the world.

ABOUT THE AUTHOR

RENEE SCARROTT is a product of the '70s who loves all things '80s. A lover of suspense and romantic fiction, Renee finds herself meeting intriguing new characters in her fictional worlds. When she's not writing, you can find her watching suspenseful movies and spending time with her uber-handy husband and their five quirky dogs in South Dakota. Please visit www.ReneeScarrott.com.